Hybrid Humans
Driven by Money and Love

Vipin Malhotra

Chennai • Bangalore

CLEVER FOX PUBLISHING
Chennai, India

Published by CLEVER FOX PUBLISHING 2024
Copyright © Vipin Malhotra 2024

All Rights Reserved.
ISBN: 978-93-56483-38-5

This book has been published with all reasonable efforts taken to make the material error-free after the consent of the author. No part of this book shall be used, reproduced in any manner whatsoever without written permission from the author, except in the case of brief quotations embodied in critical articles and reviews.

The Author of this book is solely responsible and liable for its content including but not limited to the views, representations, descriptions, statements, information, opinions and references ["Content"]. The Content of this book shall not constitute or be construed or deemed to reflect the opinion or expression of the Publisher or Editor. Neither the Publisher nor Editor endorse or approve the Content of this book or guarantee the reliability, accuracy or completeness of the Content published herein and do not make any representations or warranties of any kind, express or implied, including but not limited to the implied warranties of merchantability, fitness for a particular purpose. The Publisher and Editor shall not be liable whatsoever for any errors, omissions, whether such errors or omissions result from negligence, accident, or any other cause or claims for loss or damages of any kind, including without limitation, indirect or consequential loss or damage arising out of use, inability to use, or about the reliability, accuracy or sufficiency of the information contained in this book.

We have it in our power to begin the world over again.

— Thomas Paine

Contents

Part 1: Bring Back Love in Your Life 1

  1. Life is a Game of Love and Ignorance....................3

  2. Create Space for Love in Your Mind...................26

  3. Grow Up, Men!...37

  4. Why Has Nature Infused Love in Us?................52

  5. The Defining Spirit of Love..............................67

  6. The Two Sexes are Wired Differently 84

  7. Keep Anger on a Tight Leash...........................104

  8. Spirituality as an Expression of the Sense of Love 114

Part 2: SWEEET WILL...127

  9. Dangers of the Matural World.........................129

  10. Align With the Natural World........................152

    Appendix...186

    Notes 188

Part 1: Bring Back Love in Your Life

1

Life is a Game of Love and Ignorance

Since time immemorial, life has existed on Earth in various forms. Bacteria, plants, animals and human beings are some broad examples of the various forms in which life has existed on Earth. Within each of these broad categories, there is a tremendous variety in which life expresses itself on this planet. Today, when science has laid bare the fact that Earth is only a speck in the infinite universe and most probably it is the only planet, at least in our solar system, that has life, one cannot stop wondering as to what could be the reason for this. Is it only by chance or are we the chosen ones by God? When we observe that out of all the life forms inhabiting Earth, humans are superior in several aspects, we tend to believe that humans indeed are dearest to God. So, if we are such darlings of God, how do we explain the infinite misery that we see day in and day out in this world? The state of affairs of the world is certainly not anywhere near the heaven that we ought to deserve!

Remember that the Buddha had also ventured out of the cozy confines of his palace to find the cause of human misery. Just as in the time of the Buddha, today also all this misery is of our own making. Let us first examine closely the modern society in which we live today. Nowadays, in big cities, students study to get degrees and then pursue high-flying careers to earn money in the belief that they will be living a better life with better money at their disposal. Their schools and colleges impart specialized training to them in a variety of subjects like engineering, economics, management, accountancy, architecture, etc. Most of these subjects pertain to understanding inanimate things, such as machines, buildings, money and account books.

All this 'intelligence' instills a sense of achievement in the students and they feel empowered, looking forward to living confidently and with dignity in the society. However, slowly as they taste power, they tend to believe that earning a degree from a university not only puts a stamp of intelligence on them but makes them worldly wise too. It is this feeling that fires their ego and they start throwing their weight around. Under the influence of this false pride, s/he fails to see that her/his knowledge is only a tiny beacon of light in the infinite darkness of ignorance that every form of life has to put up with.

If we casually compare our lives with those of people in the olden days, we will immediately notice that a lot has changed. Earlier, life used to be very difficult with limited means of education, entertainment, communication, healthcare, etc. People used to yearn for better times in which there would be no dearth of schools, markets, theatres, hospitals, vehicles, etc. so that all their desires got fulfilled. Today, when we have all of them at our disposal, we are still dissatisfied and notice that this change has brought with it gifts of tension and thousands of diseases, polluted basic life-sustaining natural resources like water and air and increased family discords manifold. So, we now want to go back to Nature by investing money in eco-friendly fuels and projects. Corporate policies are being redrafted to allow employees to spend more time with their families to bring back peace in their tension-filled lives.

The point that needs to be learnt here is that most of the time, we humans believe and act in a way that we consider at a given point of time as intelligent, but later discover that we were foolish to have acted in that manner. For example, humanity first believed in God as the supreme power. Then, with the advent of the modern era, humans realized that they themselves are very powerful and can control their own destinies. So, the majority stopped worshipping God and started believing in themselves as supreme authority according to which the world needs to run. And now, we have started doubting human capabilities and believing more in the capabilities of computers.

Scientists have started working in this direction by investing heavily in superfast computers with artificial intelligence that promise to give us all the happiness and power that we have been searching for since eons! Thus, human life over the centuries may be called a long journey of acting ignorantly, without ever knowing exactly what is right for us. Some may see this change as progress but it is actually just a change in the methods employed by us to overcome extreme ignorance. In his book *Ignorance: A Global History*, Historian Peter Blurke shows how our collective not-knowing has shaped our world just as decisively as the sum of our knowledge. He goes on to say that even though our collective knowledge has grown, as individuals, we don't know much more than our historical predecessors.[1]

The faster we live our lives the higher the probability of acting in haste which later on requires reworking to mend the initial action. Today, we all are living a fast tension-filled life due to our obsession with intelligence. We are using intelligence to earn more and more money to gain recognition and quickly move up the social ladder. In the process, we are also dealing with relationships of love in haste. We are building these relationships with the sole intention of getting instant gratification and don't want to waste time on understanding and cultivating love. Money-driven logic understands instant give-and-take relationships better. This kind of relationship is mostly lust-driven and is devoid of love. This high-octane combination of lust and intelligence makes us believe, maybe in our subconscious, that LIFE is nothing but (L)ust and (I)ntelligence (F)or (E)ver.

Baba Ram Dass was right when he said, "The thinking mind is extinguished in love."[2] However, that certainly does not mean that love cannot be rekindled in such minds. Since the current generation wants to know the logic behind everything, this book will help such thinking minds to rekindle love in their lives by explaining the logic of love and how it can bring relief in their tension-filled world. It will also explain to the readers how slowing down can bring back love in their lives and at the same time, play an important role in saving the world from the mindless race of consumerism and its horrific effects on the environment.

It's not intelligence but ignorance that is the hallmark of life. Throughout our lives, we learn through mistakes, which implies that we don't even know ourselves completely. Just like the working of a high-tech machine, say a car, cannot be figured out by a layman, how can we profess to know about the complete working of the human body, along with all emotions, when it has developed over thousands of years imbibing in it the experience of trillions of situations that made it what it is today! The celebrated book *Men Are from Mars, Women Are from Venus* by John Gray is another testimony to our ignorance as it tells us that we hardly know anything about the desires and pangs of the opposite sex with whom we spend our whole lives!

Nature around us is too big and varied for us to even think of comprehending it in millions of years to come. It is almost like solving a big mathematical equation involving zillions of unknowns. All forms of life are very minute compared to gigantic natural resources that we witness around us like oceans, winds, planets, galaxies and stars. And to top it, Nature has worked so intricately in all its creations, however minute they may be, that our focus will always be limited to the immediate world around us, like that of a frog in a pond. Therefore, LIFE may well even be interpreted as (L)imited (I)n (F)ocus and (E)nergy. No form of life, as we know it today, can even think of understanding even a fraction of the vast diversity of the universe in millions of years. Because of this limitation, *ignorance is a defining feature of life* and will remain so forever.

As living beings age, they gain experience and enhance their understanding of the world around them. Then they suddenly realize one day that they have grown old and very soon it will be time for them to leave for heavenly abode i.e., all knowledge and wisdom gained by them in their entire life will suddenly come to naught one day. The future generations will start learning facts about life and the universe all over again after their exit. They will definitely have a headstart on the basis of the work accomplished by the previous generations but that would only be a drop in the ocean of knowledge that is out there to be explored. And apart from this, there is certain knowledge that can be gained only through experience. This knowledge has a kind of age lock attached to it which unlocks only when you reach that age group. You must have often heard men in their forties say that they can now understand what their parents used to say when they were young.

So, Nature has designed life in such a way that here only ignorance thrives. No living creature can be a hundred percent sure about life and its ways. All this massive evidence of ignorance flies in the face of the 'know all' attitude of the powerful that we come across in our daily lives and yet we try to emulate them in search of happiness in life. We don't realize that, to make the pain of ignorance bearable and find happiness despite it, Nature gifted life with Love. Love is that sweet emotion that fills up so beautifully the void that ignorance creates in you and allows you to relax again. Each gender fights ignorance in its own peculiar way and when two individuals of opposite gender respect each other for these peculiar capabilities and are in awe of them, romance blooms. It's a pity that in our race for money, we have ignored love and don't know how to use it for the purpose for which it was made.

It is worthwhile here to touch upon two diametrically opposed or contrasting views of life. In common parlance, these are referred to as the 'Oriental and Occidental' attitudes towards life. The Oriental or Eastern view towards work is '*Jaldi ka kaam shaitan ka*' (only people with ill will work hurriedly), while the Occidental or Western view of the same is 'Be like a duck by working like hell underneath and keeping a calm composure from outside.' While the former believes in the essence of the proverb '*Neki kar aur kuen mein dal*' (do good and forget), the latter says 'If you have it, flaunt it'. Eastern and Western lifestyles are therefore very different, even opposite at times, and this leads to lots of misconceptions.

Similarly, there are innumerable other instances of misconceptions in this world. Males have a built-in misconception about women, women have misconceptions about men, the young have misconceptions about the old and the old have misconceptions about the young. The rich have misconceptions about the poor, the poor have misconceptions about the rich, and so on. As long as we humans are not able to sort out all these misconceptions in life, we must learn to manage them through other positive alternatives that mother Nature has gifted us with, like love. If we leave it to the scientists to sort out all these misconceptions, we all would end up like the proverbial guinea pigs in the hands of the superpowerful and heartless inorganic life that scientists are currently planning to unleash on our world.

Since God is not here Himself to guide us on this wonderful emotion called love, we shall have to adopt an indirect route to understand it. Can you think of a form of life that is closest to God? Well, without a doubt it's a baby because Nature creates it with its own hand! So now, when you have a close example to follow, just try figuring out how a baby offsets its massive ignorance with love. We shall discuss the details of this later on in the book, but one thing that is clear from the above discussion is that LIFE was most probably designed by Nature to be (L)ove and (I)gnorance (F)or (E)ver. Today, when we are witnessing so much extremism and vulgarity in society, and marriages are falling apart like never before, it's evident that we have forgotten the value of love in life. Tilt towards vulgarity, meanness and extremism increases in direct proportion to our ignorance of love and its basic rules.

The manner in which we humans live our lives can be broadly divided into two categories—life that is inspired by Nature and its creations, and life that is inspired by humans and their creations. In this book, I would refer to the modern, man-made money-oriented life as *matural* life, as opposed to the natural life, the life that is aligned with Nature. Money is the essence of matural living whereas emotions are the essence of natural living. In the latter, people respect and even worship their parents, certain animals (like cows) and even stones because everything depends on the emotions attached to the person, animal or stone. They respect their parents for giving them birth and bringing them up lovingly, they respect cows because they give life-giving milk like a mother and they respect idols made of stones because they help them in remembering their deities. Hindus respect cows not only for their milk but also because the legend has it that Lord Krishna had great respect for cows. So, they can't see them being ill-treated. These are examples of emotional connections that matter a lot in natural life.

In natural life, we attach value to a person or thing on the basis of emotions attached to that person or thing. This value is very personal in nature and is love-driven. On the other hand, matural living attaches a price to a person for his/her money or money potential. It is mostly money-driven. Since natural living is on the decline, the value of emotions is on a decline and hence, love is on a decline. It is imperative, therefore, to reignite love in those individuals who have lost it somewhere in the maddening race of modern life.

A harsh current reality about the love arrangements called marriages is that they are drowning in the deluge of power and money that has surrounded us like never before. When a minuscule creation of God, riding on the blinding power of money, starts thinking of himself as a super-intelligent creature capable of amassing huge wealth-based power, he becomes incapable of accepting that he is still a small ignorant pawn in the hands of the gigantic Nature. Such inflated egos can never succeed in love, as the most basic rule in the art of love is to appreciate and value innocence. Innocence ignites love and sustains it. Kill innocence and you will kill love.

In fact, we have been killing love, in its true sense, since the time we got over-obsessed with the 'survival-of-the-fittest' attitude. This attitude has taken competition to such levels that both the mind and the environment have got polluted to levels never seen before.

In his book *Sapiens—A Brief History of Humankind*, Yuval Noah Harari says, "Unfortunately, the evolutionary perspective is an incomplete measure of success. It judges everything by the criteria of survival and reproduction, with no regard for individual suffering and happiness."

Therefore, in our quest to find what gives happiness, let us examine an interesting tool called imagination. Einstein once said, "Imagination is more important than knowledge because knowledge is limited while imagination embraces the entire world, stimulating progress, giving birth to evolution." This far-reaching power of imagination has been acknowledged by many other famous authors and thinkers as well.

To quote Harari again from his book *Sapiens*, "Any large-scale human cooperation—whether a modern state, a medieval church, an ancient city or an archaic tribe—is rooted in common myths that exist only in people's imagination…none of these things exists outside the stories that people invent and tell one another. There are no gods in the universe, no nations, no money, no human rights, no laws and no justice outside the common imagination of human beings." From this, you can easily have an idea of the massive role that stories and imagination have been playing in the lives of humans for centuries.

John Gray utilized the power of imagination to drive home the point that the two genders are so different in their mental makeup (nobody has any doubt about the physical differences!) that it seemed as if the two had landed on Earth from two different planets altogether viz. Mars and Venus.

H.L. Mencken took imagination to a new level and said, "Love is the triumph of imagination over intelligence." This is the beauty of love. Unlike logic, love has the power to bring immediate relief to troubled minds, without waiting for the results of a complex data analysis to pour in. As Einstein said, imagination is truly boundless as every human being has the power to imagine whatever s/he wants. Using this power of imagination, love creates a security blanket immediately, within which the seeker and provider can find bliss, whatever be the circumstances. This over-rationalised world of the so-called grown-ups today needs nothing as badly as the fresh cool air of imagination to bring down soaring egos and temperatures. So, let's apply some imagination to understand love and reap its benefits.

Today, scientists are of the opinion that the universe originated as a result of the Big Bang that occurred billions of years ago. Although scientists have a long way to go before they can prove this fact, we can *imagine* that God exists somewhere beyond this universe who, some billions of years ago, felt the need for a new God and the process was started by means of the Big Bang. All matter, comprising stars, planets, rivers, mountains, and so on originated from the Big Bang. When the requisite material arrangements were in place, different forms of life appeared. All living beings *together* represent the early childhood stage of this new God in the making. Since this God is in its infancy, restrictions of body and mind were kept on it. However, as an infant who always wants to break free of restrictions, we human beings also continuously yearn for freedom.

We invent, discover, fight and write to overcome these restrictions. God sought to initiate divinity in us by keeping us busy in childhood with work as well as emotions. Therefore, He made a world that had infinite scope for work and living beings with a slew of emotions like love, anger, happiness, jealousy, etc. In fact, He provided life with an infinite stock of emotions at every stage of life viz. childhood, youth, middle age and old age. Come to think of it and you will realize that a majority of the population in any society at a given point of time comprises children, women and the old who are all practically emotions personified. It's a clear indication that God wanted this world to be an extended emotional drama in which we work and feel in order to live.

The nature of work keeps on changing with the passage of time because we soon become experts in everything physical and want to try something new. That is why it is often said that 'change' is the only constant in life. What our modern society has failed to realize is that 'emotions' are another important constant of life. The same set of emotions has continued cropping up in life since time immemorial and no matter how much physically advanced we profess to have become, we have hardly progressed much when it comes to handling emotions. Time has come to focus on this constant with the same eagerness with which we are focussing on the other. They are so complex that at the point in time when we have collectively handled all possible types of emotional situations and become experts at handling them in the way that behoves a God, our childhood will end and we shall unshackle ourselves from the restrictions of body and mind. But that is not going to happen anytime soon because apart from solving misconceptions of humans among themselves, this requires sorting out differences between all forms of life. Such a future spiritual unity point would be similar to the 'Omega Point', a term coined by French Jesuit paleontologist, Pierre Teilhard de Chardin.[3]

Later on, after experiencing all the work and emotional drama over millions of years of childhood, the infant would transform into a formless God, for whom matter became redundant with the passage of time. Matter and the infinite variety of mutually conflicting situations were created in the first place only to create different restrictions that would teach the infant God to become master of all worldly knowledge and emotions. In the end, it leaves all the matter behind and goes back to the town of Gods with a reverse Big Bang. The formless God so created is invisible, enlightened and all-powerful, just like light. Our WORLD can thus be said to be a place (W)here (O)mnipotence (R)ekindled the (L)ight of (D)ivinity.

The main strength of this theory is that it treats all living beings as different expressions of the same infant God, and since all of them are in their infancy they are expected to make mistakes also. Mistakes should thus be looked upon as an integral part of the natural process of growing up of all living beings. In fact, the natural tendency of this world is to move towards chaos because that will force the infant God to realize the truth by mistakes and learn to bring back order. Further, this theory teaches us to respect others' right to live with dignity as much as ours, as we all are a part of the same infant God. Thus, it expects you to grow responsibly by learning through mistakes without threatening you with 'hell' if you don't follow a static set of rules or rewarding you with 'heaven' if you follow those rules. This theory also makes it easier to come to terms with death. Each life will go down in the memory of this future God as an experience which will be etched there forever, as a part of its upbringing.

For the future God, each life is like a tuition class that will help shape its nature. The body is like a short-term dress code required to take that particular class. When the class is over, the dress code is of no value and so is discarded, but the soul lives on, enriched by the experience gained. Thus, with death, you exit the door of limitation and carry your light (i.e. experience) to enter another door which is already illuminated with the experiences of millions of others who died before you. As infants or children are unaware of the world of adults, we are also unaware of our purpose and potential as an adult God. It seems to us that death is the end, but such vast, varied and wonderful creations of Nature couldn't possibly have been created to end up so trivially. If the wonders experienced in this boarding school called Earth are any indication, college life and the journey thereafter are definitely going to be out of this world! DEATH may thus be seen as (D)awn of (E)ternal (A)warenesss and (T)otal (H)armony.

As is the case with all children, the infant God is full of the spirit of adventure that pushes him to explore the world around him to address his feelings of insecurity as well as fulfill innumerable desires. So, to fight ignorance, he will never stop exploring the world around him and experimenting and playing with resources around him, just as a child would do with toys. Since work helps him in fighting his ignorance, he finds solace in it, and this is what the common adage 'work is worship' also seeks to convey. However, since most of the work today is based on logic, it fails to address the emotional issues. Love is needed to fill this gap. LOVE expresses itself in the feelings of a mother, father, brother, sister, children, friend, fiancé, fellow human, etc. It encompasses within it (L)ots (O)f (V)enerable (E)motions. A life sans emotions is, therefore, not possible.

Thus, love and work together help the infant fight his ignorance and give him a varied and complete experience of life. After millions of years, when this child is able to unravel the mysteries of the universe and mind, the childhood will be over and materiality will vanish with a reverse Big Bang. The grown-up God will then leave for the divine town, complete with all his experience of work and emotions. So, since God would have experienced all, he obviously would know all. That's why He is rightly referred to as Omnipotent.

The big question of how to live this life of restrictions of body and mind has foxed the infant God from the beginning. Gautam Buddha was also troubled by this question when he was young. But after extreme meditation and pain, he could solve this vexing puzzle and gift humanity with the solution in two simple words 'Middle Path.' These magical words have the answer to all the so-called insurmountable problems of life. As infant God, we are still in such early stages of growth that if we ignore the body completely, our soul will suffer due to disease, hunger and pain, and if we ignore the soul completely, as is the trend nowadays, our body will suffer due to lack of love, trust and peace of mind, resulting in addictions to liquor, drugs or even overwork. Thus, both the body and the soul need care in equal measure to live a fuller life. Clearly, therefore, we need to follow the middle path by giving equal importance to money and love in life and shunning extremism.

Such humans who follow the middle path and are driven by money as well as love in life can be rightly called

'Hybrid Humans,' just like cars that are driven by two different kinds of fuels are called hybrid cars. And just like hybrid cars, hybrid humans are eco-friendly too, because love is one of the greenest energy resources found on Earth. This is because if humans learn to utilize their love energy to care for each other and the environment, the world will automatically become a safer place to live for all species. But following the middle path is not at all easy because ignorance sparks emotions in us (like sadness, sympathy, grief, greed, etc.) and emotions easily drift us away from the middle path. An untrained mind then goes overboard and commits excesses which further generates more emotions. So, the person gets into a vicious loop out of which it's very difficult to come out. Thus, it takes a lot of discipline and courage to follow the middle path.

Extremism is raising its head in the modern world because of this lack of understanding and discipline required to follow the middle path. Once we accept the middle path as the way of life, extremism (i.e., extreme path) automatically becomes meaningless. Extremism also becomes meaningless if ignorance is accepted as the basic truth of life, because then you know that you can't be hundred percent right in everything you believe in, and the other person can't be hundred percent wrong in everything he believes in. The saying 'Excess of everything is bad' also seeks to convey the message that extreme action must be avoided as it doesn't bring any good.

The world is today hurtling towards self-destruction due to climate change and nobody knows how to slow it down, given the enormous costs involved. Several green measures are being adopted to save the world from the increasing level of carbon dioxide in the atmosphere that is causing climate change. These measures include increasing the use of solar energy to produce electricity, increasing forest cover on Earth, decreasing the use of fossil fuels, and so on. However, unless the breed of hybrid humans takes over this responsibility in right earnest, nothing much can be achieved by governmental action alone to slow down our mad race towards self-destruction.

There is a desperate need to save humans from themselves as they have happily given in to greed and forgotten the *sense of love* that they have in them from birth. They need to be taught that their fellow human beings are a different experience of the same infant God and must be treated with the same dignity and respect as we expect for ourselves from others. Today, when we all are busy outsmarting each other in making increasingly intelligent and interactive machines, where do you think man's quest will stop?

Obviously, after getting engrossed in his machines to the core and neglecting his family completely, he would like to produce a machine with which he can share his fears and anxieties too. As per newspaper reports, this process has already started with research into Artificial Social Intelligence (ASI) recently taking off in some countries. The next step would obviously be to build a machine that cares for and understands the human who owns it. So, smart devices of today will slowly graduate to emotional devices. What do you think the most advanced version of such a machine would be? Obviously, a manufactured human! We are trying to work towards a world that is already there! Such is our ignorance that, instead of trying to respect fellow humans for their emotions, we are trying to physically rebuild them, complete with all social skills and emotions! It would be far wiser for us to make efforts to increase our understanding of human nature and its potential in this field rather than wasting millions of dollars on artificial intelligence and generating an equally massive e-waste in the process.

Ignorance is a defining feature of life and no matter how much more we may work, with any speed whatsoever, this feature will stay with life forever. In our pursuit of power, we have not even achieved the power to move at the speed of light yet. When do you think will we be in a position to make planet-sized machines roaming effortlessly with perfect time periods in an infinitely expanding physical space? We have to realize that Nature has infinite wealth and infinite speed. Are we going to rest only after achieving this infinite power of Nature? How many lives do you think would it require for us to catch up with the power of Nature? So, if life is about so much ignorance and there is no point in speeding away to be as powerful as Nature, why not slow down a bit and allow the infant God in its early childhood to witness all the beautiful emotions that accompany a relaxed life?

Slowing down is also the most pressing need of the modern world which is working overtime to dig its own grave by usurping all natural resources at breakneck speed. In a recent interview, the UN secretary general, Antonio Guterres, said that the world is consuming 1.6 times the resources available for consumption on the planet today.[4] We all need to seriously deliberate how long our planet can support life if we go at this rate. And since there is no planet B ready for us yet to migrate to, we don't have any choice but to slow down. Remember, despite the gigantic size of this universe and the comparatively negligible size of life forms, Nature has worked so intricately while creating life forms that every individual of every species lives in a world of his/her own. Everybody is fighting his or her own battle to make sense of this world having infinite variety and perspectives. That's why it takes time for an individual to understand another individual. Therefore, time is important for love to blossom and so slowing down is an important prerequisite for valuing love in life. A hybrid human would understand this and help slow down this hyperactive world by spreading awareness about love and its benefits.

At the launch ceremony of the World Happiness Report 2023, Jeffrey Sachs, co-author of the report, said, "Virtue, ethics and happiness in our ancient traditions of Plato and Aristotle or Christianity or Buddhism or Hinduism or other great ancient wisdom, went hand in hand with the idea that to be happy was a skill that one developed by being a good person. Aristotle explained that being a good person meant being good to oneself and to others. We forgot a lot of that in modern history. The ancient tradition was brushed aside by some bad philosophy of Hobbes and others, who said, people are evil, nasty, ruthlessly ambitious, insatiable in demands and it's all a game of power or wealth…".[5]

This game of power and wealth has brought us today to the brink. We saw in this chapter that life is a very different game, so it's time to understand the essence of the teachings of old great philosophies and cultivate a sense of love for fellow human beings and all flora and fauna. Under the harmful philosophies of the last few hundred years, we have killed this sense in us which is so vital in creating sustainable lifestyles. In this book, we shall learn how to restore that sense as well as feeling of love in our lives and in the process save the infant God from the threat of annihilation brought in by our over-obsession with competition.

2

Create Space for Love in Your Mind

Love is an emotion which gives you security. You feel protected as it reaches out to you by default without any precondition like a mother reaches out to a child. Its reverse is a cut-throat competition where you work to make others insecure by promoting your own interests without any remorse, like one business entity does to another in the same industry. Today, technology has given us so many tools in our hands that we are literally overwhelmed by their sheer power and speed. And with such power and speed, these tools obviously help everybody earn more.

Since money is something whose reach is understood by one and all, the whole human race today is engrossed in remorseless competition, fuelled by the rapid strides of technology in countless fields. This vicious nexus of money and technology is working overtime to make rats out of humans. It weans away humans from emotions like love and respect, and at times makes them indulge in shameless displays of greed to such an extent that what is left behind is a travesty of humanity.

Every active member of every family is busy learning the use of his/her own set of tools. So, anybody who is a part of this endless race doesn't have the time to think of other needs of the human body. Hence, although today's education is producing good professionals, this has at the same time resulted in making wisdom the biggest casualty. The simple reason for this is that the student is left with no time to pursue this *unprofitable* goal, the demands of his profession and consumerist society being so big. But the result is there for all to see. Rapes, divorces, murders, mass shootings, suicides, pre-marital cohabitation, extra-marital relationships, etc. are tell-tale examples of a confused society whose members lack the basic wisdom of what is right for them and what is not.

Today, we are so blinded by the money-generating power of the tools provided by technology that while looking for an opportunity to earn money, we are prepared to even indulge in deceit and dishonesty with our close relations. This happens because money-driven logic is accustomed to giving importance to something in accordance with its monetary value. And since relationships cannot be valued this way, we assume them to be relatively low in importance. Also, in order to earn money, we regularly practice cold logic in our business dealings and inadvertently get into the habit of getting cold to some extent in our emotional dealings as well. All this results in the neglect of emotional bonds.

Neglect means not fulfilling each other's aspirations, the purpose for which you are in a relationship. Hence, neglecting a relationship tantamounts to dishonesty. Over an extended period of time, this habit firms up and dishonesty starts showing up in our dealings with everybody. Why else do you think the warmth or closeness that used to be the hallmark of relationships between blood relations, neighbours or friends has slowly given way to mere formal niceties? It is because of this neglect or dishonesty in relationships that has crept in owing to the money-driven logic.

Money-driven logic has this nasty habit of reducing the most beautiful gifts of Nature, like love and innocence, to the level of dirt. It is the 'I-am-not-paid-to-be-nice' kind of attitude that has sounded the death knell for warmth in relationships and replaced it with bluntness and rudeness, which, if allowed to go unchecked, takes no time to graduate into ruthlessness. And this unemotional culture unleashed by money on the psyche of the current crop of homo sapiens has left us emotionally so bankrupt that innocence and honesty are afraid to spread their wings lest they get mauled by the fangs of this monster. The worst affected by this onslaught are of course the soft targets viz. children, women and old parents.

Do you remember when Bollywood or Hollywood last came up with a lullaby or a song in celebration of childhood's quintessential innocence? You can very well have an idea about the fading away of those honest feelings of love nowadays from the fact that the songs being churned out today pale into insignificance so quickly 'vis-à-vis' the catchy love songs of yesteryears which are still etched in our minds. Doesn't it reflect the degradation of the emotional quality of our society as a whole? When old parents are bundled up and kicked into old-age homes, money-driven logic revels in finding the best solution for them because it is unable to comprehend the pain of shattered emotions.

Nowadays, maximisation of shareholder's/self-wealth is the guiding principle of corporates and individuals. All emotional relations usually fall by the wayside when the attainment of this goal is at stake. If not by overt means, then by covert means, nobody hesitates in making a quick buck at the cost of others. Today, the equation, *wealth = peace of mind*, makes perfect sense to all of us. And in the process, wisdom has taken the worst beating ever because excess wealth is usually accumulated by overlooking emotions. In the older days, when consumerism had not yet afflicted society and excess wealth was conspicuous by its absence, emotional sacrifices used to be the rule rather than the exception. WISDOM used to come early in those days because we get the gift of wisdom (W)hen (I)ntense (S)acrifices/sufferings (D)evelop (O)ur (M)ind. You will notice that wisdom is usually associated with elder members of any society precisely because of this reason, i.e. their long exposure to emotional turbulences in life makes them wiser. Intelligent people just manage machines while wise people manage far superior and complex machines called humans.

Let us now try to understand whether money, by itself, is bad. Does it really wean human beings away from humanity? We all know very well that apart from providing us with our daily bread and butter, it opens up a flood of opportunities of several kinds and in the process, brings hope in several lives. It brings a feeling of security. It brings mobility and employment. So money, by itself, cannot be termed bad. It is our attitude towards it that puts it in a bad light. Money has the power to *win* materialistic battles. It puts you into the habit of *winning* or acquiring materialistic possessions. It has the power to remove materialistic poverty. That is why it generates such awe. It is rightly said that man is a creature of habits, but when this habit of winning trespasses into the emotional arena, money starts doing the damage for which it is notorious.

With money, you can get materialistic satisfaction, not emotional. In the matter of relationships, happiness comes through mutual warmth and that in turn comes by 'giving,' a concept that is alien to money. Rather, it's exactly opposite to the basic tenet of money viz. profit making. Money fails in its role of a 'Winner' in matters of love because emotions are not its forte. It's like asking Sachin Tendulkar to build a skyscraper. You can trust money to build a fortune for you but it is naive to expect it to build emotional bonds. This is the crux of the problem that our society is facing today. The rules of earning big money push you to become self-centered and emotionally dishonest, whereas the essence of love, as described in the following pages, lies in honesty.

Money-minded people need time off for special training or conditioning to cultivate respect for relationships and vice versa. It is not by coincidence that hardly any businessman has ever been a good poet or hardly ever a good poet has been a good businessman. The persons who have single-mindedly devoted themselves to earning money have destroyed their love life and those who have single-mindedly pursued love have lived in penury.

The culture of 'dishonesty pays,' as discussed above, when combined with the fact that everybody is short of time nowadays, lays down the ideal atmosphere for the modern-day youth to have little or no feelings about the feelings of their fellow human beings. This trend is visible everywhere in the world today and it can be reversed only if we are able to learn to spare time and then spend that time to understand the importance of love in life. For a start, we can take inspiration from the Mother Earth herself. Since time immemorial, she has never tried to rush things by attempting to complete one rotation in less than 24 hours and a revolution in less than 365 days. When we work overtime, we are attempting to finish work before its time, unlike Mother Earth. Working overtime as a habit is a matural work culture, obviously not in tune with the rules of Nature. It overtaxes your mind and body, leading to abnormal behaviour and health risk. Claudia Goldin, the winner of Nobel Prize for Economics 2023 calls such work 'greedy work' and identifies this kind of work as one of the main reasons that is hindering pay parity among male and female workers.[6] Thus, one big change that our work culture today needs is to banish working overtime from our lives. This will help us in investing our spare time to fulfill the equally important non-monetary expectations that our family has of us.

There is a limit up to which money can make the quality of life better. If allowed to go unchecked, MONEY can become a (M)aze (O)f (N)ever (E)nding (Y)earnings. Those who run after money to seek happiness and security have a very simplistic view of life. Life is a long emotional drama involving various emotions. It is not only about happiness and security but also about sadness, pain, anxiety and a host of other emotions. Nobody has ever been able to run away from these emotions, however hard s/he may have tried. But everybody willfully closes his/her eyes to this truth and wants to keep himself/herself busy with the unending chase for money, hoping that it will magically solve all their problems one day.

However, closing eyes to a problem has never solved it, whereas facing it has often thrown up surprisingly simple solutions. For example, by accepting the fact that drinking and driving don't mix, you can save yourself and your family a lot of trouble by simply asking someone else to drive when you are drunk. Similarly, we need to *accept* that money is not going to solve all our problems. It plays that role up to a certain limit and beyond that, it simply corrupts the mind and the body. When (MON)ey (S)tarts (T)rivializing (E)motional (R)elationships, you should know that you have reached your limit after which it will turn you into a MONSTER.

The Annual World Happiness Report 2023 has placed Finland at the very top in terms of happiness sixth time in a row. When a professor at the University of Eastern Finland was asked to comment, he said, "Finns derive satisfaction from leading sustainable lives and perceive financial success as being able to identify and meet basic needs."[7] So, *everybody has to set his/her own limit for his/her financial needs.*

To improve the quality of life after crossing this limit, we need to create space for love in our intensely money-focused minds. Science has not yet been able to decipher the working of the human mind, but so many poets and spiritual leaders have long been able to bring peace to innumerable lives by using imagination. It has been proved beyond doubt that stories have the potential to change our view of life and bring peace within. So, let me also relate a story to prove a point.

This is an old story about two friends, one of whom is a goldsmith and the other is a florist. One day, the florist invites the goldsmith to his home for dinner and when he comes, he shows him his collection of beautiful flowers. But the goldsmith simply tests them on his touchstone and declares that they are of no value. The florist gets the shock of his life but remains mum. Then one day when the goldsmith calls the florist to his home and very eagerly shows him his collection of jewels, it is the turn of the goldsmith to get shocked as the florist goes about sniffing at each piece of jewelry and declares that they are of no value as none carries any fragrance whatsoever.

By the same analogy, when we go about searching for the fragrance of life while keeping our mind focused on money alone, we meet failure. The rise in violence, vulgarity, marital discords and suicides today indirectly reflects this failure of money to provide that fragrance in life which comes from the flower of love. The first step required to grow this flower is to learn to shift some of your focus from money to love in your mind because the flower of love grows on the soil of your mind.

To get a hint of what the presence of love in your mind can deliver, you just need to visit a temple, mosque, church or any other place of worship. You will automatically feel the tranquility and benevolence of the place bringing peace to your mind. If such is the power of a single visit, then you can well imagine the power of spirituality that the scriptures talk of! It's a big failure of our education system that it ignored the priceless treasure of love and values stored in our sacred scriptures and instead bombarded our young students with materialistic concepts so much so that they consider our ancient values of love and respect for each other an outdated concept which is of no relevance to the modern world.

This has happened because our education system is totally career-oriented, with its roots in the 'survival-of-the-fittest' theory of the West. This approach creates a halo around 'power,' thereby making wisdom an expendable irritant in the pursuit of power. Today, the degrees being awarded by our education system are trying to camouflage our basic nature i.e., ignorance. On getting a degree, a student is designated as an expert which fuels his ego so much that he mocks at the word 'ignorance.' This kills humility in him and he starts dictating rather than listening. When an ignorant man dictates, the result has to be chaotic, and love and respect are the first casualties.

The assumption of leaving it to the parents to teach the concepts of love and respect to their children has failed miserably and the time has come to formally educate our young generation on the importance of these values in making and keeping us humans. The parents obviously have not been able to cope with the volley of questions asked by the young mind that is trained for seeking logic behind everything, especially in the East where the old generation has been forced to go on the back foot by the culture shock unleashed by Western education. This is because the parents were brought up on faith, a synonym for love. They had faith in their parents who in turn had in theirs, and so on. Family values were thus passed down from generations mostly on the basis of respect and faith only. The logic was generally conspicuous by its absence.

In this part of the book, an attempt has been made to logically explain the traditional belief that even when two unknown souls are tied in a nuptial knot, they can convert it into a lifelong relationship if the rules of love are followed in the right spirit. These rules will help you create space for love and innocence in your mind, and they, in turn, will help you connect more with the soul than the body.

3

Grow Up, Men!

*A*sk any man as to what could be the possible reason behind the pleasure that all living beings experience from sex. The majority of them will immediately come up with a ready answer, "The natural compulsion for procreation is the obvious reason. Nature wanted to ensure the continuation of species on Earth by making sex a pleasurable activity. " And they go on to add, "So, there is nothing wrong if a man thinks about sex umpteen times during the course of a day. After all, he is being perfectly natural." But what after that? What about the delicate new soul who comes into being as a result of this perfectly natural act? "Well, money and womenfolk are there to take care of it" is the prompt answer. So, in a nutshell, most men tend to think, "Men were made to impregnate women and provide them with the necessary wherewithal, while women were made to bring up the child with love and care." However outrageous it may sound, this is the prevailing truth about the knowledge of gender roles of most men.

The question that begs an answer from such men is, is that all about life and its beauty? What about love? Where does that come into the picture? The job of impregnating a woman can be done as well by lust as by love. So, how is love different from lust? Or, is love only a figment of the imagination of womenfolk and of those men who are not macho enough to face the might of the brute and the invincible? Unfortunately, more often than not, these questions are left abegging in most lives! Nobody has the time to venture into this unprofitable territory. So, men keep on behaving like landlords and women keep on behaving like their property and both keep on existing like this throughout their lives, missing out on one of the most beautiful gifts of Nature, viz. love.

However, with the dawn of modern education, men have been made to realize in no uncertain terms by women that they can earn as well as men, if not better, to provide the necessary wherewithal for bringing up the child. So, now most men have gone on the defensive, trying to fish out one or the other reason to justify their existence. The realization that they are not the superior sex has dealt a telling blow to their psyche. Till now, this mentality had led them to believe that women were meant to be controlled by them and that they were the final decision-makers about their lives.

They firmly believed that womenfolk had to follow the directives of menfolk and that women represented that part of the human population which had to spend their entire life looking up to their men for everything. Hence, they are now trying to retaliate by challenging the fairer sex with strange theories like equality of sexes in physical terms too and in various other ways that are leading to physical and mental torture of the fairer sex. Thus, we are witnessing a sharp increase in the cases of broken homes and bestial behaviour towards the fairer sex.

So, let us first try to figure out why men have been behaving the way they are for ages. It is obvious that a man has more physical strength than a woman. So he was in a better position to win all physical wars and battles. This fact filled him up with pride and women sought refuge under powerful men to protect themselves from vandals. Women reciprocated this gesture of goodwill of men by what came to them naturally viz. love, affection and care. Men misinterpreted this gesture of submission by women as their weakness (because that is the way men judge other men) and thought it fit to limit their freedom in order to protect them from harm.

They believed that any man can take advantage of women due to their looks and their physical and emotional vulnerability. This laid the foundation for the rock-solid belief of men that they themselves were far superior to women and that the womenfolk should better subscribe to the dictates of their menfolk to live life with dignity. Purposely or otherwise, men kept women away from education and made women economically dependent on them as it helped them in their scheme of things.

The human body is such that it can be moulded in whatever way we desire, physically as well as mentally. Men or women who do intense physical labour get equipped to do many things which seem impossible to a person who has advanced mental abilities and vice versa. For example, a labourer may be able to carry so much weight on his head as an office-goer may not be able to carry in his hands. Why does this happen? Because the former has moulded his body to be physically strong while the latter has moulded it to make it mentally strong. And there are millions of physical and mental qualities to which this body can be made accustomed to. That is the beauty of Nature. Nature has blessed this world with so much variety that, if we try, we can keep discovering infinite newer varieties with the passage of time. But there's a catch. When we accustom our body to a particular thinking process, we tend to get carried away with it. We regard it as the ultimate truth of life and vehemently oppose any efforts by anyone to challenge it and change it.

In his book, *The Seven Spiritual Laws of Success*, Deepak Chopra rightly said, "Human beings are nothing but bundles of conditioned responses." Anything that goes against their age-old beliefs is opposed tooth and nail by them. The history of mankind is replete with innumerable such instances to prove this. Everybody knows that when Copernicus floated his Heliocentric theory against the Geocentric theory about the movement of planets, what a storm it raised! The intense hatred of staunch believers of one religion towards those of others is another important example to prove this fact. But why do you think wise men have always said that one should hate badness and not bad men? It is simply because the bad man is behaving in a bad way because of bad influences. If the effect of these influences withers away, we will get a good man. This is the power of influences on the human body! So, we should always keep ourselves open for changes in understanding and hence, attitudes.

Till the time life was simple, the old gender roles worked very well with men getting contented with the assumed submissive nature of women and women content with looking after the home and showering love and affection on family members. But with the advent of modern education, stress is now more on the development of mental faculties as opposed to physical strength. Since in the ultimate scheme of things of Nature, women were never intended to be slaves of men but in fact, the two were supposed to move hand in hand with each other, the mental faculties of the two were kept on par by Nature. Hence, modern education has smashed to smithereens the age-old belief of men that they are superior to women. But, this has also led to the opening of the proverbial Pandora's Box. Men, who have got their thinking process moulded in an ancient way, are unable to accept this revelation and hence, they are opposing it with whatever they can lay their hands on.

To add to this confusion is the fact that modern education is totally capitalist in its outlook. The most sacred thing for it in life is profit and so, only those ideas are preferred and pursued that have the potential to earn profit. Profit is the key to survival. This mentality has made men with Western education fiercely materialistic. They tend to pursue the give-and-take policy in relationships too. Emotions are anathema to them. Respecting a person for the sake of a relationship doesn't make much sense to them. 'Respect' compels you to look for positive points in the behaviour of the other individual and overlook his/her negative points. But this goes against the very grain of profitability, for if you keep respecting a person, you will never be able to make money from him. Hence, respect for the sake of 'intangibles' like behaviour, age, relation, gender, etc. has been bid adieu by such individuals.

Society is therefore witnessing now a growing tribe of men fed on modern concepts of core profitability who respect others only for the sake of money or power (the bad philosophy of Hobbes and his ilk is hardly showing any signs of ebbing out). Since emotions like love and respect slow down the race towards both, these smart young worthies usually keep them at bay. Emotions are seen as a hurdle. When this man faces intense competition from the fairer sex, the result is a highly insecure male who has all his missiles drawn up to attack (physically, monetarily and/or emotionally) at the first signs of opposition from any person of any age or any gender, whether related or not.

Such a highly charged-up male loves to take his inspiration from wild beasts like a lion or tiger and prides in being compared with them rather than feeling a sense of shame in it. He is not able to realize that the majority of the population in the society comprises children, women and old persons and all of them look for love and understanding from him, not a show of animalistic strength. His misconceived notions about love and emotions are further fuelled by the business community, which considers such a man a big asset as he is a fierce fighter. He is capable of earning them loads of money by demolishing the competition. So, today there is no dearth of men who are proud to be crass and materialistic and enjoy showing the fairer sex down for having dared to step into their territory. Eve teasing, usage of highly sexist abuses, and rapes are some of the methods employed by them to do this.

The kind of male that we discussed above is zero in relationships. He is, more often than not, attracted to the opposite sex due to his sexual desire and not emotional desire. Due to biological reasons (scientists have shown that the hormone, testosterone, in a male's blood compels him to think about sex several times in a day), he is attracted towards the opposite sex but because of the moulded thinking he comes to acquire due to excessive exposure to exploits of power, his attraction is devoid of feelings of love and full of gain motive. This kind of attraction is called lust. All men have this in varying doses. But a man who takes the modern style of living a bit too seriously suffers acutely from this affliction.

This would have given you a fairly clear picture of the way an overly money-minded modern male thinks about the opposite sex. He is drawn to her more with lust rather than love. Further, due to the insecurity/jealousy generated by her professional success, he often tries to obstruct/restrict her progress. This insecurity has a lot to do with the patriarchal society that we have been living in since ages in which power has been grossly overrated and worshiped. As society has undergone a change in modern times, the modern male should realize that for a happy life, he must desist from always using power to deal with opposition.

He should learn to appreciate the emotional nature of women. Then only it would be possible for the two genders to complement each other. He must learn to value the feeling of care and belongingness that a woman has for her family. While the man is busy grappling with the outside world, the woman literally feeds the children with her body and feelings. She weeps with them and laughs with them. But for all this, she needs full support from her husband and here is where the trouble begins. By facing the big bad world outside and being largely ignorant of the female mind, the modern male usually starts seeing motives in all her moves.

Instead of giving her a free hand with his honest support, he starts competing with her or uses force to make her follow his dictates. He sees his home also as a shadow of the outer world. But this is not the proper perspective for building intimacy at home. A man needs to be mature enough to keep a delicate approach at home and realize that with power comes responsibilities too. A happy home cannot be built on the basis of power and strength alone. It requires a dynamic mix of power and emotions. The more men mature and understand the opposite gender from a proper perspective, the easier it would be for them to be at peace with themselves and the world.

Martin Luther King Jr. once said, "Our scientific power has outrun our spiritual power, we have guided missiles but misguided men." It is hoped that this book will make the men understand the opposite sex better so that they become capable to provide the women and children the ideal atmosphere to blossom in the safe haven of their homes and give the harried old parents the gift of second childhood in their twilight years.

Now, it has become easier to understand what we always suspected. Men who value love are usually more content with their lives vis-à-vis the men who don't but are otherwise go-getters and movers. The former give and get love and care whereas the latter keep on searching for this elusive contentment in every other thing. For getting every other thing you need money. So, they run after money ferociously. They can go to any extent to earn that extra buck because they are never content with the life they have got.

They appear to be all over and to be doing all the work. The businessmen go gaga over them and they are richly rewarded. They thus become the heroes and the trendsetters. But money, by nature, is very addictive. So, such people keep on running after money for the sake of money alone and never get something for which they started this race in the first place. To quench their thirst for money they are prepared to go several extra miles. Hence this character becomes street-smart.

Denis Healey was right when he said, "It's easy to be brilliant if you are not bothered about being right." That's why such a man seems to be winning more than a person who has learnt to fall in love. Hence, to the uninitiated and foolish, a nice person looks boring vis-à-vis the other person who is street-smart. Today, the popularity and material success of these street-smarts is a direct indication of the level of awareness of love in our society.

Such persons become exploitative by nature and intense lust for sex is one of the by-products of this exploiting mentality. Also, as a direct consequence of cut-throat competition, they don't feel secure in the company of anyone and as a result, they do not feel at home anywhere. In fact, they no longer relate to the word 'home' in its true sense. The institution of marriage and home, and the culture of respect for the fairer sex are becoming a target of this exploitative nature in males leading to a tremendous rise in marital discords.

In her book *The Will to Change: Men, Masculinity and Love*, the activist and thinker bell hooks says, "Boys are shamed out of their emotional vulnerability, and they cover up this suffering with rage, with the mask of masculinity."[8]

Males need to wake up from the wrong notions of masculinity instilled in them by the patriarchal society and concentrate positively on the emotional nature of the fairer sex. It is these emotions which play a major role in making the fairer sex lovely. So, those who see its flip side i.e., jealousy, moodiness, talkativeness, etc. hate women for their emotions and those who concentrate on the positive side, love them for being so opposite, almost like a child.

There is an old Hindi song penned by Indivar in the film *Qurbani* that states this fact so beautifully:

> *Mohabbat ka jisko tarikka naa aaya, usse zindagi ka salika naa aaya*
>
> *Raah-e-vafaa me jaan par jo khela, uske liye hai ye hasino ka mela*

The second line of this couplet seeks to convey that a woman is at her loveliest when she is assured of unconditional honest support from her lover, a kind of 'till-death-do-us-part' commitment. Remember that women keep the same kind of commitment to their children, as is evident from the fabled mother-child love witnessed around the world for ages. Commitment is in her nature and so she appreciates and respects the person who has it in good measure. So, when a male wants a fruitful relationship, he must not only expect commitment from her but should be ready to reciprocate the gesture, whatever the circumstances.

A smart man thus enjoys this lovely creation of God by first appreciating the 'opposite' in the 'opposite sex' and not the other way round. A relationship has slim chances of survival if it is misdirected from the start. Men who approach the opposite sex driven only by sex remain boys forever, with the marital bliss playing hide-and-seek with them all their life.

In her article 'Great Expectations' in *Times of India*, Narayani Ganesh says, "It is sexual desire driven by lust which leads to violence against women. This never happens when there is compassion, love and respect."[9] Any trace of violence in a marital relationship is a clear sign of a lack of love, understanding and maturity, and it must be addressed with urgency.

John Keats famously said, "A thing of beauty is a joy forever," but, as someone else has rightly said, a man usually tends to think that a woman is a *thing* of beauty and he is a *boy* forever!

A famous sexologist once said, "Men offer love to women to have sex and women offer sex to men to be loved." The #MeToo movement and the demand for legislation for ban on marital rape in several countries also point to the compelling nature of sexual lust in men. Therefore, high levels of understanding and maturity are required on the part of men to tame this lust. Gender education can greatly prevent clueless boys from begging and looting something that can be managed with some love and understanding.

The contribution of men to the making of the matural world has been phenomenal, but their role in devastating the natural world is no less. And one of the major factors that contributed to this devastation has been their inability to understand and include women in the making of the matural world. Even today, educated and smart women like the former prime minister, Jacinda Ardern, of New Zealand and the former Scottish first minister, Nicola Sturgeon, have chosen to resign from their posts because they wanted to step away from the brutality of modern politics.[10] On the recent social media spat between the world's two richest men, Elon Musk and Mark Zuckerberg, where one tweeted "I'm up for a cage match if he is" and the other responded by asking him to send the location for the fight, a leading daily came up with an editorial having similar title as of this chapter. It said that the time has come "to raise the bar for men. They should not be rewarded for acting like children who break things to get their way. The wreckage of such behaviour is writ large all across Earth."[11]

So, it's high time for the menfolk to grow up and understand womenfolk so that a kinder society can be built. Gender education at the school and college levels can help bridge this gap because, to quote Historian Peter Burke again from his book *Ignorance: A Global History*, "women's knowledge has been hidden from history for most of the time. Their contributions to the arts and sciences have been disregarded, their own ways of knowing have been disparaged, creating blind spots in human knowledge."[12] The two genders will have to move together in their onward journey in order to prevent an apocalypse in the not-so-distant future. This book is a small effort to address these age-old misunderstandings between the two genders by prodding them to follow the middle path, which is the path of love. One of the reasons for this long-standing misunderstanding could also be the insufficiency of language in dealing with emotional issues. Again, this is partly due to the fact that it has been largely a man's world till now and so emotional aspects were not properly developed in the language.

The recent inclusion of emojis in our day-to-day texting is a right step in this direction as they are able to convey emotions better than words. Another medium that has been used for ages to convey emotions is music. Poetry with music has often been acknowledged to convey emotions better than plain prose. Therefore, in this book, you will sometimes find references to some extraordinary examples of poetry which, along with catchy music, have touched the hearts of millions over the years since their creation.

4

Why Has Nature Infused Love in Us?

Have you ever wondered why our education system teaches us everything except love? There is no separate book on love and there is no separate tutorial on love in schools and colleges, even once a week. I think this total blackout on one of the greatest human needs has converted this world into a theatre of the absurd rather than a school for divinity (as discussed in Chapter 1). The education system today, focused as it is on physical sciences, convinces a student that if s/he dares, everything in this world is attainable, and money and technology have the power to make this possible.

What it fails to teach is that human beings are not 'things.' They have emotions. And hence to attain happiness in a close relationship, the principles that apply to money will not work. The term 'love' today merely signifies a word that is used only to promote one's image in society in the hope of gaining some material benefit out of it or simply to look 'cool' in society. Thus, by not touching this subject at the school or college level, we are leaving our students as half-baked adults.

There is an urgent need to understand, accept and teach the truth mentioned in the first line of the couplet from the song of the Hindi film *Qurbani* that was mentioned in the previous chapter:

> *Mohabbat ka jisko tarikka naa aaya,*
> *Usse zindagi ka salika naa aaya*

In simple words, it states that one who doesn't know how to love doesn't know how to live. Due to a lack of clarity on love, today's youth are wildly experimenting with various concepts of dubious records such as live-in relationships, speed dating, etc., and in the process giving in to their basic desire of seeking happiness/pleasure from a relationship in the rawest form. So, they are in urgent need of education that polishes and refines their desires. Love education must be a part of gender education. It will refine their basic instincts and make them understand the difference between love and lust more clearly. This will enable them to approach the opposite gender more appropriately.

In my opinion, the theory of soul mates being made in heaven for each other, a common theme in most movies, is floated by naive people and, of course, by those who have vested interests in it. The former have left everything in the hands of God and the latter, like movie makers, stand to profit by playing this game. There is a chance, however, that one may genuinely love a person at some point in life and consider him her soul mate, but to expect the same honest feeling of love being reciprocated is usually the stuff that fairy tales are made of. It hardly ever occurs in real life. So, education can help one find his/her life partner faster and with confidence.

The unabashed consumerism that we are witnessing in society today is a direct indication of the emotionless life that the majority of us have chosen to live. As we have started giving more importance to consumer items and less to humans, it's only natural that today we understand these items more than humans. By blindly surrounding ourselves with maximum consumer items, we are simply betraying our human disconnect. This gives birth to insecurities and infinite desires for one-upmanship that in turn leads us to that eternal competition in which we get busy competing with each other full-time, and in the process forget the basic human traits. This attitude degrades relationships over time and a spiritual void starts building up within us.

The following translation of a poem, originally composed by me in Hindi, gives an idea as to what a person misses in life if he/she remains devoid of love. For those who are interested in reading the original poem, the same is given in the Appendix.

Importance of Love in Life

Love provides honest support
Love makes you feel others your own
Love induces interest in life
Which is multiplied further by love alone

Whoever remains devoid of love
Feels helpless and his life becomes a load to tow
For him all colours of life fade away
And his own breath becomes his own foe

His life becomes deserted
The whole world looks like a cremation bed
He searches for the reason to live
And wanders like a living dead

That's why somebody has rightly laid this fact bare
That love is God and love is prayer
Love is not useless, it's the basic need of all humankind
It alone brings a hearty smile on your face and peace in your mind

The stream of life meanders due to love
Without love a person becomes pitiable
Love alone has kept hope alive in this world
Without it, life becomes a mockery and regrettable

Relationships of love are the base on which this world stands
By ignoring them you may earn a lot but, at heart, you stay alone
The umbrella of love gives the cool shade
Desired by everybody since times unknown

Friends, love is so infinite, it's impossible to write down its full glory
For the time being, just understand, without it life gets miserable

> So, even by mistake, don't ever belittle love in life
>
> Because love alone makes this world colourful and livable

The above poem must have helped you to gauge the importance of love as a subject of study. It is precisely for this reason that we are going to dig deeper into this subject in this chapter. This book intends to provide a basic time-tested working model for man-woman relationships that can be used by one and all, whether married or still searching for a soulmate. The model will help to initiate a life-long partnership or to mend a deteriorating relationship of a couple who are at their wit's end to save their marriage. It may be mentioned here that religion is also a working model which gave peace of mind to a local community at a particular point in time. Hence, religion is localized by definition and as such, it makes perfect sense locally only.

In this age of globalization, when cities are turning into big metropolises, we need to accept this localized nature of religion. Unless we do so, we will not be able to create the right kind of atmosphere for people from different parts of the world to exchange ideas and progress collectively. Hence, a change in attitude and maturity of thought are needed for the collective good of all. Similarly, a change in attitude is needed by the two sexes towards each other as well for leading a more meaningful and contented life. That is exactly what this working model strives to achieve in this book.

We already know from the previous pages that ignorance is the hallmark of life and emotional drama is one of the main features of life on Earth. One of the most important ways Nature ensured this was by creating two genders of almost all species on Earth and making them mentally and physically very opposite, but at the same time linked their destinies in such a way that they cannot find fulfillment without each other. This arrangement of ignorance about self as well as the opposite gender on the one hand, and their dependence on each other for fulfillment on the other hand, ensures the continuation of life-drama on Earth for eternity.

Let us now try to understand the different natures of the two genders by taking a closer look at the different creations of Nature. We find that on the one hand, Nature has created large oceans, horrendous jungles, huge mountains and an infinite universe while on the other hand, it has created such tender beings like rabbits, fishes, kittens and of course, little human babies. In addition, there are old and sick beings who are equally vulnerable. Hence, Nature intended to be soft as well as hard in its creations. So, the two genders were so conceptualized that one would admire, nourish and support all that is tender and beautiful in this world and the other would explore and unravel the harsh, the horrible and the invincible. However, if both genders follow their own individual interests and do not interact with each other, the very purpose of having two genders of a species is defeated because then they can very well be individuals of two different species altogether. Therefore, Nature made the continuation of a species possible only when the two genders come together and cohabitate.

To make the cohabitation fruitful, it was necessary for the two genders to feel the need for each other. This need could be kindled only when the harder of the two genders searches and gets the soft experience from the other, and the softer of the two genders searches and gets relief from the harder experiences through the other. So, then Nature created this need for each other in the two genders and simultaneously created that beautiful emotion called love which would fulfill that need by bringing the two genders together and binding them in a beautiful bond. *Love is therefore Nature's age-old idea of getting fulfillment and happiness.* By this arrangement, Nature ensured that everybody who loves is able to appreciate both soft as well as hard experiences of life and, therefore, treads the middle path.

Remember that since it's destined to be a middle path, there will be challenges also but love will help conquer these challenges and spread happiness. All other ideas of lasting happiness are matural and hardly ever pass the test of time. The matural promise of getting life-long happiness/bliss is too far-fetched and utterly unnatural. It is promised by naive people or those with vested interests having a gain motive. No happiness dependent on the material world is permanent because change is the only constant in the material world. As our knowledge expands, the material world keeps on changing and with it changes our idea of happiness.

As mentioned in Chapter 1, emotions are another important constant in the living world in the sense that they are within all living beings as long as they are alive. So, they can possibly become the source of permanent happiness. We have just seen that the one emotion that was designed exclusively by Nature to provide happiness to living beings was love. So, can love provide life-long happiness? The answer is a big yes. Love is indeed that source of happiness that brings along with it the stamp of permanence if we follow the rules as explained in the following pages.

From our discussion of the 'natural gender roles' in the working model discussed above, we can conclude that Nature intended men to make this world a better and easier place to live in and it made women to make this world a better and lovelier place to live in so that they could together complement each other and enjoy this journey of life. However, since exceptions exist in every facet of life, the above generalization of gender roles is also subject to exceptions. When Nature assigns different roles to its creations, we should learn to respect the difference rather than resist it. Like Nature assigned the trees a task opposite to that of living beings. Trees are natural food-producing factories that inhale carbon dioxide and exhale oxygen whereas living beings do exactly the opposite. So, they complement each other's existence. However, today we have built factories that inhale oxygen and exhale carbon dioxide like us. The result is unprecedented pollution that is killing us slowly. The race for equality between the two sexes that modern life has unleashed is also polluting young minds against each other. The two opposite genders are like the two opposite poles of a battery cell. When the two opposite poles are connected to a bulb by wires, the bulb glows due to the current flowing between the two opposite poles. However, if the cell happens to have similar poles, the bulb will not glow because of lack of current between the two poles. Similarly, life looses its glow when the current of love stops flowing between the two opposite genders when they strive to compete with each other and become similar in thought and action.

What immediately follows from the above discussion is that both sexes have different sets of commandments from Nature to make this world a better place to live in and so their approach to various issues of the world has to be naturally different. The male of the species was gifted with inbuilt predatory instincts to push the known frontiers and a matching body, mind and brain to protect and defend himself and those under his protection from the consequences of such action, even in extreme circumstances. Similarly, the female of the species was gifted with an inbuilt instinct for nurturing with a sense of belongingness and a matching body, mind and brain to provide wholehearted support to those she considers her own, even under extreme circumstances.

It's strange that the staunch supporters of the 'survival-of-the-fittest' theory are supporting the race of equality of sexes and denying in the process the very theory they want to propagate. The natural process of creating two different genders in each life form must have survived the millions of years since the birth of life on Earth only because it was the fittest way for every life form. In fact, it is the best example of the 'survival-of-the-fittest' theory. The two genders are no doubt equal in importance in the natural scheme of things but both have very opposite attributes. So, the competition for one-upmanship being witnessed between them in the modern world is downright ridiculous. Instead of competing with each other, they should be contributing to each other's success and, in the process, completing each other. This is in conformity with the concept of optimum utilization of resources in order to maximize benefits and minimize wastage of resources. By realising and utilizing their opposite natural potential, the two genders can bring peace in their lives and do away with avoidable mental stress. In fact, here I am reminded of the evergreen song of the Hindi film *Hamraaz* that was released in 1967. In the melodious voice of late Mahendra Kapoor, it describes so beautifully how love is played out in Nature in different ways in order to sustain each other. The song goes like this:

> *Neele Gagan ke tale, dharti ka pyar pale*
>
> *Aise hi jag mein hoti hai subah, aise hi shaam dhale*
>
> *Shabnam ke moti, phoolon pe bikhren, dono ki aas phale*
>
> *Balkhati belen, masti mein khelen, perhon se milke gale.....*

This can be loosely translated into English as 'Under the blue sky, day and night, love is witnessed on Earth in several ways. Like, the dew drops spread out on flowers to fill each others' wish. Similarly, vines seem to be going wild with fun when they swing on the trunk around which they are growing...'

In her article 'Shiv as Ardhnarishwar' in *Times of India*, Alka Nigam writes that studies show that everybody experiences two types of consciousness in their inner core—as male or female. This duality faces existential problems, because the unconscious part of the self, whether male or female, desires to experience itself as a whole. She further writes that Indic philosophy has long conceived of the divine reality as both male and female. This abstract idea is captured in concrete in the idol of Ardhnarishwar, showing the right half of the body as God Shiv and the left half as Goddess Parvati, in union. She says that the concept of Ardhnarishwar can be defined as the totality that lies beyond duality. The Swiss psychoanalyst, Carl Jung, called these two unconscious parts of the mind as Anima and Animus. He says that Animus, the unconscious masculine side of a woman, manifests qualities of a male as thoughtful, assertive, powerful, and wise. Likewise, the qualities of Anima like tenderness, kindness, patience, and the desire for nurturing are often manifested by men. Their innate traits, however, are not conflicting but complementary to each other, implying that a completely balanced personality is possible by adopting the missing characteristics.[13]

Love helps you find this balance in life by letting you adopt a person that has these missing characteristics. Wisdom lies in accepting the fact that the two genders are wired differently and so both have a different approach to life. Women's approach tends to be more in the nature of caring and sharing whereas men tend to be more cold and analytical in their approach to resolving worldly matters. So, in a way, both complement each other by focusing on those aspects of life that are not the focus of the other.

Traditionally, the emotional intelligence of women has been better than males due to a variety of reasons, their physical vulnerability being one of them. We have seen far more men becoming seers by retiring to jungles to meditate as compared to women, primarily because men could disconnect with their families more easily than women and women could understand the emotional needs of children and elders in the family better. This might have also happened due to traditional patriarchal arrangements in a society wherein boys are indoctrinated from childhood to suppress their emotions. Whatever the reason, the difference in gender behaviour over the centuries the world over is too stark to ignore. It's ironic, however, that it is this difference in approach which usually becomes the bone of contention between the two sexes. This happens when we fail to realize that owing to the divine design discussed in the model given above, a 'better' solution will almost always be the one that has the consent of both sexes. And to make that possible, it is imperative for both sexes to appropriately understand the nature of each other's needs.

There are many facts about the behaviour of men and women that can be explained on the basis of their 'natural roles' discussed above. For example, men can now understand why women, being the guardian of all that is soft and tender, bring grace and manners in whichever field they venture into. Similarly, women can now understand why men like these gestures but hardly ever follow them because, for them, action lies somewhere else. We will study in detail many other conclusions that can be drawn from this working model in Chapter 6 of this book.

Change in the attitude of the two sexes towards each other is the goal of this book and it requires inculcating new ideas. So, allow these new ideas to sink in slowly and experience their power thereafter when they merge with your nature to show you a whole new world where each creation of Nature fits in so beautifully. After all, ideas rule the world and the mind. Beautiful ideas make you a beautiful person and crooked ideas make you look crooked in other's eyes and leave your ownself unfulfilled. As discussed before, change is an indisputable truth of life and so change in outlook is possible but you will have to exercise the necessary will to bring that about.

5

The Defining Spirit of Love

*I*f the two genders have to cohabit, then, naturally, the next step is to set up a place of cohabitation where the two can live with love. We, humans, call such a place home. So, we shall study about home and love in this chapter. Where else to start our learning of these two concepts than from that period in our life when we all get introduced to them? So, let us now analyse our childhood atmosphere. It won't be difficult because almost all adults cherish their childhood memories the most, which are kept close to the heart as a treasure. On recollecting those memories, you will realize that the following factors acted simultaneously to provide you with the best experience of your life. No doubt there were several other factors but the following five will suffice for our study:

(a) Forgive and forget attitude among family members for anything and everything (after usual fights and deliberations)

(b) Emotional security

(c) Blind trust in all family members

(d) Eulogizing each other quite often

(e) Clearly defined career work i.e., going to school

How may one describe a home? A home can be described as a place where you get complete emotional satisfaction. When the atmosphere in your house becomes such that you are unconsciously convinced at the back of your mind that the family members have a forget-and-forgive attitude towards each other (factor (a)), albeit after some verbal exchange of views, your house gets the *basic ingredient* to become a home.

Now, let us come to the all-important question, how can we describe love? Well, according to the ancient Indian saint Kabir, the answer certainly does not lie in books. He had this to say:

Pothi parh parh jug mooa, pandit bhaya na koye,

Dhai akhar prem ke, parhe so pandit hoye.

This couplet can be loosely translated into English as:

The person who has understood the meaning of love stands taller,

Than the one who has mastered countless books and becomes a scholar.

The Defining Spirit of Love

Since the answer does not lie in books, it must lie in experience. That is why we have set out in this chapter to analyse our childhood experience. Out of the five childhood factors listed above, we have discussed on the previous page the role of the first factor (a) in the making of a home. Now, if we can bring about factor (b) and factor (c) into play in our homes, with a generous sprinkling of factor (d) every now and then, we come very near to the childhood scenario. Factor (b) comes when your relationship with your spouse is able to radiate such confidence in him/her that he/she believes that you are there to listen to his/her wildest of fears/dreams and you will not belittle him/her for that or make a mockery of his/her thoughts/feelings. Your mere presence automatically works as a support system for him/her. And the ultimate success of factor (b) is measured by the fact that it graduates into factor (c).

Remember that it is the level of honesty in your support system that determines the achievement of factor (c) in your relationships. Once this factor (c) is achieved, you will suddenly realize that 'love' is the only word that comes closest to describing this relationship. So we can safely conclude that the *defining spirit* behind love can be expressed in two words viz. 'Honest Support.' With time, your loved one will feel your personality radiate that divine charm called love.

This fact can be corroborated by thinking about the loveliest thing that God created on Earth. It is very commonly seen and our reaction to it is so spontaneous that usually, we don't realize while interacting with it that it is the loveliest creation of God. It is a baby! By just looking at a baby you will feel like kissing it and spending some time playing with it. Have you ever wondered why this happens? Why does a baby look so lovely? It is her innocence which works on you. And what is innocence? It is the ignorance of the world's ways that leads to an uninhibited show of emotions by her [factor (b)] and blind trust reposed by her on you that you will do her no harm [factor (c)].

So, we again conclude that when factor (b) starts working in your relationships and reaches its pinnacle by achieving the level of factor (c), the warmth of love starts radiating, much the same way as the magic of a baby works, and we experience love. Thus, 'Honest Support' kick-starts love in life. Love has often been said to be blind. Factor (c) in our analysis vindicates this belief. Truly, love is not love unless it has the power to overlook the mistakes of the loved one. The last factor in our above analysis i.e. factor (e) is being given prime importance by our education system today. A paying career certainly helps in attaining factor (c) by taking care of the worries of food, clothing, shelter, medicine, etc. but, as pointed out in Chapter 2, only up to a certain limit!

Since times unknown, poets have been describing different facets of love. Our aim above has been to understand the defining spirit behind love so that we can understand such descriptions better and enjoy the glory of love in a more fulfilling manner. But make no mistake here that honesty in your support doesn't come automatically. It may be so for some time but sooner or later, it requires conscious effort and maturity on your part to maintain it that way. Beginning of most relationships are honest, but as time passes, life throws up innumerable situations where your support system is put to the test. It is a very fine art to keep the right balance in your behaviour so that the defining spirit behind love never extinguishes. It goes without saying that time is of great essence in this relationship as the feeling of honest intentions sinks into a human mind only when it can pass the test of time consistently.

The sweetness of any relationship is directly dependent upon the level of honesty in it. For relationships, honesty is still the best policy and will always be. In fact, this spirit holds good for all kinds of love, be it motherly, fatherly, sisterly, brotherly and of course, that of a spouse. Love takes different hues depending on how it is expressed. In this part of the book, we are concentrating on the relationship with one's spouse because it is the source of all relationships, in the sense that it leads to the creation of a home which, in turn, is the birthplace of all other sweet relationships that form a family. So, now that we know how to cultivate love, we can bring about love in our lives instead of squarely blaming luck for the lack of love in our life. It is a hundred percent achievable and not with somebody specially destined by the Almighty for you but with anybody and at any age. Dream men and women are not custom-made by God for you but the partners themselves customize each other by learning to cater to each other's needs over a period of time.

Of course, it helps immensely if the person chosen has the consent of your family because it saves you a lot of time and energy to attenuate the hurt feelings/egos of your immediate family members. In these highly challenging and exhaustingly competitive times, when time has become a rare commodity, it certainly makes sense not to initiate this ultimate relationship of honesty and trust on the ruins of other relationships of the same nature. You may also note from the above analysis that love and home complement each other and that's why their definitions are also intertwined. There is a complex web of emotional relationships that complement and supplement the two. Hence, to obtain the best results, the two should not be viewed in isolation. Another point that is worth noting from the above analysis is that the defining spirit behind love is 'giving' honest support. Hence, the *essence of love lies in giving rather than demanding*. However, if the spirit of giving is not mutual between the two partners, there is every possibility of the single source drying up early. Thus, to keep the relationship vibrant and alive this feeling of 'giving' should be in both the partners.

Needless to say, to be able to give, you need to possess a 'large heart' and that requires courage of the highest order if seen from the point of view of a profit maker. This can probably explain why a profiteer always views love with disdain ("It's all nonsense" sort of stuff) and a lover always doubts the intentions of a profiteer when he/she suddenly claims to have undergone a change of heart.

None other than Mahatma Gandhi once said, "A coward is incapable of exhibiting love. It's the prerogative of the brave," and "The weak can never forgive. Forgiveness is the attribute of the strong." Lack of 'large heartedness' keeps our thought process narrow and inculcates in us the bad habit of judging others even on frivolous issues. This usually acts as a springboard that lands us in the quicksand of the eternal blame game.

The Love Cycle

In order to promote meaningful life on Earth, Nature created the Love Cycle just as it created various other cycles about which we have read in our school textbooks, like the oxygen cycle, water cycle, rock cycle and so on. The love cycle works as shown in Figure 1 on next page.

Hybrid Humans

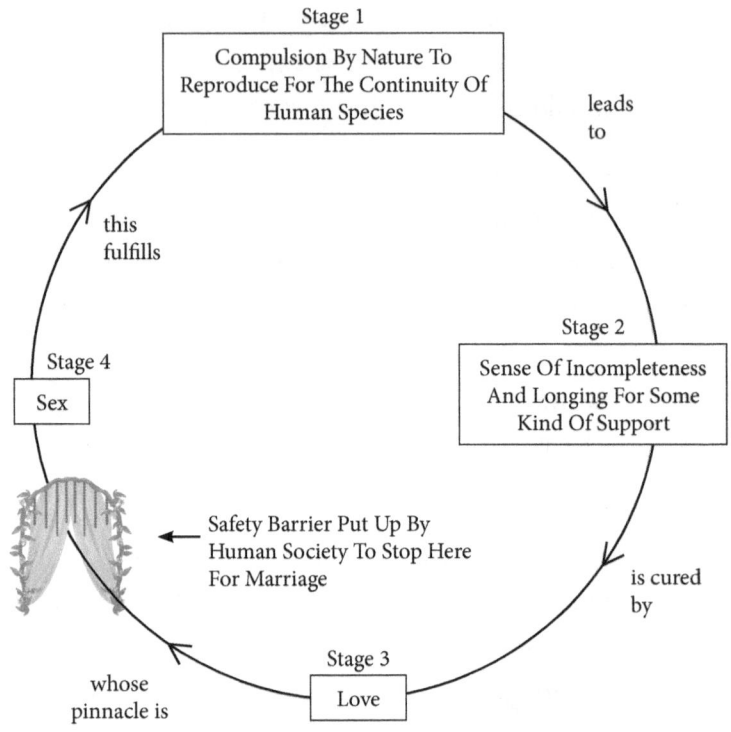

Figure 1: Love Cycle

Image (wedding gate) credit: <a href='https://pngtree.com/freepng/arch-wedding-decoration_6685384.html'>png image from pngtree.com/</a>

Stage 1 of the love cycle is self-explanatory in the sense that infant God would be able to survive only if it has the ability to live forever or it is able to reproduce. Since the former option is not available, the compulsion to reproduce is present in all forms of life, including humans. Stage 2 depicts what we discussed in Chapter 4—Nature created the need for each other between the two genders by creating a sense of incompleteness in each of them. The age-old concept of Ardhnarishwar and the existence of Anima and Animus, as suggested by Carl Jung, testify to the existence of this sense of incompleteness due to which duality seeks totality.

We further discussed in Chapter 4 that, simultaneously, to fulfill this need and bind the two genders in a beautiful bond, Nature created love. This is depicted in stage 3. In her book *A Room Of One's Own,* Virginia Woolf talks about the androgynous mind—that perfect state of being when the female and male consciousness embrace in harmony. She says, "When this fusion takes place, the mind is fully fertilized and uses all its faculties. Perhaps a mind that is purely masculine cannot create, any more than a mind that is purely feminine."[14] Love has the ability to create such a fully fertilized mind that uses all its faculties. So, love is the third and the most important stage of the love cycle as it brings peace to troubled minds. Thereafter, when two loving souls unite, they complete the cycle through stage 4.

In the above cycle, we can see that between the third and fourth stages i.e., between love and sex, the human society has put up a safety barrier to stop for marriage. Earlier, marriage was held between stages 2 and 3 but now, due to increased intermingling of the two sexes in society, its position looks more appropriate between stages 3 and 4. This change in positioning, however, doesn't make much of a difference if the rules of love are followed in the right spirit. This safety step was taken by our forefathers because they knew that sex is meaningful only when it is with one's spouse. Otherwise, the support that we talked about while defining the spirit behind love in the previous pages no longer remains honest. And the support which is not honest, as discussed, cannot be love. Extra-marital or pre-marital sex defeats the very purpose for which Nature created love. Sooner or later, it will rear its head to haunt your married life. Hence, to enjoy the fruits of love, one must adhere to the rules of the love cycle depicted in Figure 1. The discipline of the love cycle carries more importance today when the power of money has come into young immature hands and personality disorders leading to loneliness, depression, suicides, etc. have reached epidemic proportions.

Marriage brings with it many other advantages. Apart from providing legal sanction to the union, it unconsciously trains us in the art of giving, which is so necessary to cultivate love. So, what seems like a barrier to the unversed is actually a gateway to a contented life. Usually, with marriage comes a whole new family for the bride as well as the groom. This provides the ideal platform where we learn to respect the viewpoints and needs of persons who might have been total strangers till now. Emotions of various hues come into play in a joint family and teach you when to put others' emotions before your own and thereby learn to sacrifice for others.

For example, when an old grandparent asks for help in standing up or sitting down, slowly but surely you realize that his/her requirement is more urgent than yours and you learn to attend to him/her first. You will realize over a period of time how even small acts of help/giving bring happiness and forge emotional bonds. Sacrifice and love are closely related. Where there is sacrifice, bonding is automatic. Such wise inbuilt mechanisms in the institution of marriage inculcate the habit of giving. The lack of these mechanisms in modern nuclear families is contributing immensely to the rising intolerance in society leading to the drifting apart of close relationships.

Marriage, therefore, can be viewed as that seed of relationships from which grows the plant that bears flowers of love of different hues when it is nurtured with the water of honesty over a period of time. If this plant is well-nurtured, it spreads the fragrance of life and eventually grows into a tree that provides cool shade for a lifetime and fruits of the most delectable kind. Sadly, however, most people nowadays are too lost in the jungle of a materialistic world, run by logic and competition and ruled by money, that they are simply unaware of the existence of the soft and caring world of innocence and love, or they are too stressed out to spare any time to go into the finer aspects of this seemingly unprofitable nonsense called honesty.

In either case, the water being given to the sapling of relationship sprouting from marriage starts reeking of dishonesty leading to the drying up of the plant from the contamination and after a short period, all that is left is the foul smell emanating from the dead flowers of love. Young couples should take up marriage with the sincerity of a startup. Unless the requisite effort is put into making them work, marriages will keep failing like any startup that lacks sincerity in efforts. Remember that man is a social animal and so a healthy network is a must for every human to bide his/her time fruitfully on this planet. Wisdom lies in making relationships emanating from marriage a very important part of that healthy network.

An important conclusion that can be drawn from the love cycle, besides many others, is that sex is an intimate and private affair between life partners. The public portrayal of a sexy image is, therefore, as pointlessly enticing as a mirage in a desert. It is a fad promoted by the fashion and film industry to laugh their way to the bank at the cost of the unsuspecting general public, who sometimes pay for it by inviting loneliness, depression and miserable loveless life. Striving to become 'lovely' (for her) or 'chivalrous' (for him) is a far better goal to pursue to attract genuine relationships. Instead of experimenting with sex, experiment with love. The same goes for advocates of sex education in schools. Instead of educating about sex, educate about love because sex is only a small part of the whole cycle of love.

As we just saw, both the love cycle and childhood analysis help us in building a home full of love. For the best results, it can even be said that if a man's loyalty and faith in his spouse has the honesty of a father and similarly a woman's loyalty and faith in her spouse has the honesty of a mother, then that would provide the ideal atmosphere for a life-long relationship of love between the two. The closeness between two partners, whose relationship has its foundations laid on honesty, is enhanced by leaps and bounds by physical touch. An occasional reassuring non-sexual touch can work wonders in a relationship. As a sample, just try giving a hug or two to your spouse and you will see positive results showing up very soon.

Similarly, try appreciating him/her by saying "I love you for that" or "I am proud of you" as frequently as you can and you will feel mutual warmth building up slowly to give shape to your sweet home. Other small ways that can help forge better soul-to-soul contact can be as simple as sipping a cup of tea together after a day's hard work or sitting together and sharing the day's experiences with each other. Your eyes play a very important role in relationships. Love is a divine language that is read through the eyes. Formal languages are no match for it. Love conveyed through eyes is much more honest and satisfying than that conveyed through gifts, because money cannot be trusted whereas honest emotions expressed through eyes seal the trust.

Today, society is more busy with material hunting rather than love hunting. This has led to a loss of faith in family bonding among young children too. This is clearly evident from the rise in juvenile crimes and increasing haughtiness in the behaviour of children. Schools and colleges are imparting technical education and the study of the working of the human mind and emotions is negligible. This gap leaves the students confused as many questions about life and relationships that they have remain unanswered. The child is taught that all confusion can be dispelled by excelling in academics because then he can earn as much as he wants and spend at his own wish to get whatever he wishes in life. So, the very basis for excelling is laid down on monetary benefits. The child of course imbibes it in letter and spirit and ventures on this misdirected goal. The unexplained questions about life and love in such children show up in their behaviour in various forms such as silence, loneliness, anger, violence and so on.

So, when he grows up, he tries to search for his inner peace in money and works his heart out for it. Simultaneously, he gives vent to his love desires through random lust-driven physical relationships. But where does all this take him? Inadequate time spent at home leads to weak relationships and working like a machine at the office gives him ill health. Random physical relationships become an additional irritant. So he suffers both mentally as well as physically but since his unequivocal devotion to work earns him laurels for being an excellent workman, he hardly ever complains. Although this lifestyle doesn't provide him with the warmth and closeness of relationships and gives him ill health to boot, he doesn't complain because he has enough money to indulge in all materialistic comforts, pleasures and medication! Slowly, he gets addicted to the power of money and works only to earn more and more money so much so that many a time earning money alone becomes the purpose of his life.

But, being a human, he feels emptiness sooner or later in his life and feels the need to share his inner feelings with somebody. Although he again tries to kill this feeling by indulging in such diversions as shopping, dining and wining, entering into live-in relationships, etc., with increased vigour but fails. At this point, he has reached the second stage of the love cycle. Hence, we see that this lust for money has delayed his arrival to the second stage of the love cycle. This is the problem with the materialistic lust that the present education system is inculcating in students. Directing them on the path of materialistic excellence is delaying and in extreme cases even killing the onset of the second stage of the love cycle in them. And since one lust feeds on the other, such children get addicted to sexual lust more easily and take a shortcut to bypass the third stage of the love cycle. As a result, they land directly on the fourth stage and complete the love cycle *minus* its most important component viz. love (see the incomplete or truncated love cycle given in Figure 2 below).

So now, can you understand why for many young people sex has become synonymous with love today, even after marriage? There is an urgent need to

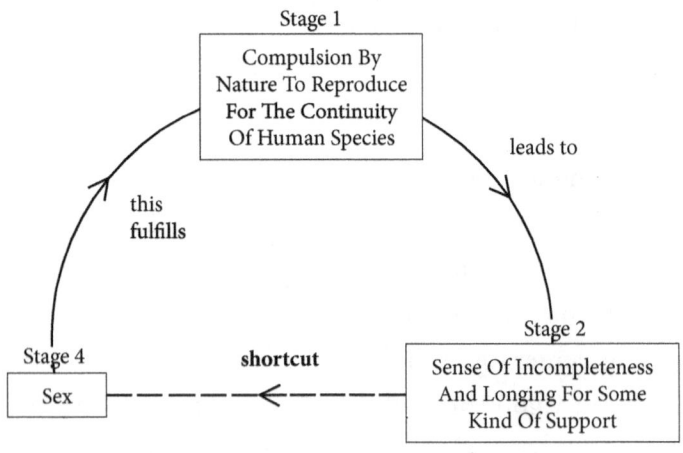

Figure 2: Truncated Love Cycle

prevent young men and women from indulging in such shortcuts. They need to be taught that love has a deeper meaning and is not limited to just a pleasure act! We will also see in the second part of the book how humanity as a whole is going to pay a very heavy price because of this habit of taking shortcuts.

6

The Two Sexes are Wired Differently

*S*cientists have found that, on an average, women's brains are highly connected across the left and right hemispheres, whereas the connections are typically stronger between the front and back regions in men's brains. Similarly, we know that during adolescence many bodily changes take place in the two genders. One of the more visible changes is that a man's body hardens and a woman's body softens. Just as the body structures of the two sexes are different, even opposite in some respects, their thinking processes are also different, even opposite at times. We shall now look at some of these differences and use the model just discussed by us to aid our understanding. At the outset, let me first state the not-so-obvious fact that it is this difference in body and outlook that sets the basis of romance between the two sexes. More the difference, the more the attraction, but also the more the chances of misunderstandings! That's why a grown-up man-woman relationship is not child's play. Precisely because of this, we are going to take a closer peek at some of the basic traits of the two sexes in the following pages in an effort to make this relationship a romantic encounter that lasts for a lifetime.

The whole idea of masculinity is today enveloped in layers and layers of artificiality. Somebody rightly said, "Nothing prevents us from being natural so much as the desire to appear so." It is largely this urge of covering ourselves up to appear normal that has led to artificiality in relationships. Due to the traditional patriarchal setup of society, the majority of men that we come across today believe that expressing suffering somehow weakens their position in their peer group and that's why, tragically, they avoid being seen as suffering. By silently suffering, they keep on building up the pressure within. These pent-up feelings show up in their behaviour through some other route. In some, they lead to diseases like depression and in others, they sow the seeds of anger and violence.

In her book, *On Violence and On Violence Against Women*, the philosopher Jacqueline Rose writes, "No man comfortably possesses masculinity, and it is this discomfort with one's own human vulnerability that rears its head as the delusion of mastery, as contempt for weakness." She identifies an erotic charge, an obscene pleasure in the license to violence in men.[15] But Nature never intended to be cruel to the infant God during its upbringing. Nature knew that living beings would suffer mentally for various reasons due to ignorance and so it provided a ready antidote for it in the form of opposite gender.

Men and women are natural antidotes to each other's suffering. They can effortlessly provide each other with much-needed relief from stress in everyday life. However, more often than not, the male's misunderstood manliness comes in the way and reminds him that it is a weakness to look weak. That's why men have traditionally tried to keep their distance from emotions, have seen women as weakness personified and looked down upon them as one of those three Ws (wealth, wine and women). Their common refrain has been that it's very difficult to understand women and so, many of them don't even give it a try. The two genders are so different from each other that it is easier for each gender to misunderstand the other than to spend time to understand the real reason.

When men went to battlefields to fight horrible wars or when they went to deep jungles to understand the meaning of life, women preferred to stay at home and fight every day in a lonely battle to give love and care to vulnerable family members. Men misunderstood their preference for home as their weakness, and since they were more powerful of the two, their interpretation prevailed and relegated womenfolk to the background. Men's inability to understand women unconsciously led them to concentrate more on their physical beauty. As a result, they started treating women at par with pleasure-giving 'objects' like wealth and wine, and hardly ever listened to a woman's advice. In the process, men also suffered and women suffered because of them.

When boys grow up into male adults in a patriarchal society, they discover from their interactions with grown-up men (or rather, grown-up boys) that the first rule of survival in their gender is to give emotions a back seat and let their decisions be influenced purely by the logic of gain, be it in terms of money, muscle power or pleasure. Since money leads to more power, the 'natural role' of making the world a 'better and easier place to live in' is interpreted by most men as having more and more money and clout. (Recall the 'natural gender roles' we arrived at in the model we discussed in Chapter 4.) That way they get immediate recognition and respect from other members of this gender. Why do you think it's difficult to be a gentleman today and why is modesty considered a liability rather than an asset? It is simply because gentlemen do not seem to exude power and are therefore considered weak! So, you will find a majority of men trying to play to the gallery and become materially successful rather than finding time to listen to the emotional SOS of their families. It requires great grit and determination to become and stay a gentleman nowadays.

To quote Jacqueline Rose again from her book *On Violence and On Violence Against Women*, "Many forms of supremacist thinking, domination and hierarchy are linked. But men are not the problem: the problem is our collective investment in masculinity as superiority and prowess. Men and women internalize patriarchy because we live within that system, but both men and women can resist it."[16] It is true that both men and women can resist the patriarchal system but, as I said, it requires great grit and determination to do that. The patriarchal system is surviving till now because not many could gather the requisite courage to resist it. Most people adopt the easy way out and join the system, thus further strengthening its roots.

As a boy grows up, his primary aim is to establish himself as a man in his peer group. As emotions pull him back from achieving this goal quickly, he slowly starts getting into a state of mind where anything related to emotions looks unmanly to him. Hence, the innocence in him slowly starts giving way to the cut-throat logic of gain. The Western lifestyle, which gives undue importance to the profit mentality, hastens up this alienation from emotions. At this stage, intense raw lust for sexual pleasure also starts building up in boys. This basic instinct is usually so compelling that many of them find an outlet by keeping illicit sexual relations. It is not for nothing that prostitution is regarded as the oldest profession in the history of humankind. And to top it, unabashed support for sex by the business world today, because of their firm belief that 'sex sells everything else,' helps build up his preference in favour of sex vis-a-vis love during these formative years.

The businessman (being a man himself) knows very well how to capitalize on the basic instincts of men. Using various means, including media, he fans sexual lust to push forward materialistic lust and fans materialistic lust to push forward sexual lust. The two lusts work hand in hand to keep the cash registers of the businessman ringing. So, for the uninitiated, it is imperative to understand the intense money-seeking philosophy of the pied piper called a businessman who will, by all means at his disposal, try to pipe his way to the bank even if that means reducing you to the level of one of the rats in the hopelessly meaningless rat race.

Slowly, the word 'pleasure' starts looking more meaningful to boys vis-à-vis 'love' because the former has a prospect of gain in it, without any liability. The fast stressful life of today also gives impetus to this thought process because, under such circumstances, a person seeks an outlet through instant gratification which is provided to him by illicit sexual relations or pornography. It is for this reason that fast sex, like fast food, has become the latest fad in contemporary society. But it needs to be remembered that both are detrimental to health. Just as the latter makes the body sick, the former makes the soul sick because people indulging in it are effectively bypassing the third stage of the love cycle, jumping straight from the second stage to the fourth stage. They fail to realize that it is the third stage which gifts them with that elixir of life that awakens the soul to the presence of the charming world of innocence and love all around it.

It is often said that the first love of a girl is usually her father who pampers her to no-end and makes her feel like a princess with his whole-hearted love and care. This innocent idea of love stays with most girls all their life. They inadvertently look for these qualities in their dream boy also. Nature's idea of loveliness can be experienced in its full glory when a woman smiles with all positive emotions displayed leisurely over her beautiful face and eyes full of dreams about a man for which she is ready to submit her whole self for a lifetime. Thus, in order to facilitate women in their 'natural role' to make this world a 'better and lovelier place to live in', Nature has blessed the fairer sex with an abundance of emotions with the requisite faith and strength to go to any lengths to care for their loved ones.

As a result, we find that in almost all cultures it is the girl who leaves her parent's house after marriage for the sake of her man and adopts his family also, because the essence of love lies in giving rather than acquiring. Females can get very deeply involved emotionally and it is this factor that plays a key role in keeping relations alive. The famous proverb, "Hell hath no fury like a woman scorned," also testifies to the presence of a very high level of emotional quotient in females. It is this emotional strength that makes them an ideal candidate to bind two families together after marriage.

However, it is almost impossible for a mind obsessed with money-making to appreciate the spirit underlying this act of love. For this reason, in many societies, a woman is penalized for this supreme act of love by her in-laws, who demand dowry as a trade-off! She is looked down upon, humiliated and subjected to untold oppression for her sacrifice. How infinitely dumb! Ill-informed men and women view this sacrifice as her compulsion for getting security for life in the power-worshipping society built, controlled and regulated by powerful men. Such people only betray their deep entrenchment in the archaic patriarchal system.

It is a fact that a woman is physically less powerful than her opposite gender, which makes her physically vulnerable. So, she needs emotional validation before moving forward in any relationship. As a result, emotions take a front seat in a woman's life. And rightly so! If women have to do justice to their 'natural role' of nurturing all that is soft and vulnerable in this world, they need to have a firsthand experience of the same themselves. Spontaneous acts of love and care can come only when there is a deep understanding within, through experience and/or birth. Herein lies the dilemma of being a woman. The 'natural role' assigned to them by Nature has placed women themselves in a vulnerable position. Wrong notions on sexual behaviour have made the saviour herself the hunted!

As seen above, since emotions are deeply ingrained in women, they get emotional quite often. An emotional outburst in which you want to pour your heart out or an emotional reassurance in which you want to feel contented in your heart requires a very well-developed knack to make yourself heard and also hear out others. Hence, women love to talk things out to relieve their emotional stress and encourage others also to do the same to help them out. Now, imagine you are in an alien place surrounded by strangers. Your biggest need at such a place is to feel protected and if you get the same in the form of respect and acceptance, your confidence level immediately shoots up prompting you to come up into your best form. This same transformation happens in a woman who gets vibes of love from her in-laws and her husband. Women glow on being cherished as that transforms them magically into their 'natural role'.

Recent research findings show that children's relationship with their mothers is of more warmth and more conflict.

Clearly, therefore, females relate more closely with children. Their body and voice also remain soft to enable them to relate with children realistically. With such physiological traits and a very emotional nature, women are generally a lot more soft-hearted vis-à-vis men. The patriarchal setup of society enhances this difference further.

This is a very important difference between the two genders that men choose to ignore day in and day out and get away with it due to the power that they wield in the predominantly men-driven society that we currently have. Men continue to be ruthless and harsh in their behaviour with women most of the time, without even realizing it. That is why, as said before, there is an urgent need for gender education to make the two genders appreciate each other rather than hate each other due to mutual ignorance of each other's ways.

By this arrangement of keeping women soft in body and thought, Nature has provided in a woman a close confidant of a child. As a result, the strongest emotional bond that we can witness on Earth is that of a mother and child. Nature is never artificial in its creations. When it chose woman to nurture and give birth to a new life, it ensured in her all the essentials required to create a home viz. a place of ultimate intimacy. These included soft emotions like love and care, jealousy, belongingness, alogic, insecurity, beauty and innocence in good measure.

Note that all these things are found in good measure in a child as well. So the two are natural allies and go on to give the home the bliss of intimacy. It is also because of this arrangement that women have the tendency to become brattish when subjected to harsh treatment, whether physically or mentally. If the man of the house is large hearted and gives her the maximum space between the expanse of his arms, both experience a mutually satisfying experience.

In this over-rationalised world built up by men over the last few centuries, technological advancement has been grossly overrated. Without understanding the role of women in the natural scheme of things, men have been busy building the matural world where progress has become synonymous with technological advancement. Men have been seeking to make a 'better' world by wholly concentrating on technology. They have tended to ignore the fact that Nature has also assigned women the task of making a 'better' world. They never allowed women to use their intelligence to interpret 'better' in their own unique manner.

Intelligence is one aspect in which men and women do not differ at all. Since Nature has put equal responsibility on the shoulders of men and women to make this a better world, the level of intelligence in the two sexes was kept equal so that they can meet at the same level of intelligence and complement each other to make it a better world. However, this would be possible only if both are given equal opportunities to prove themselves. Not giving equal opportunities to girls is a heinous crime because that makes the softer gender more vulnerable. As a result, instead of fulfilling her natural role of being the protector of the rights of the vulnerable, she herself becomes a target for no fault of hers. And it is precisely for this reason that women have remained oppressed for centuries.

Ignorant of these facts, while growing up most boys start believing that the ways of women will take them nowhere. They are in a hurry to learn the 'ways of the world' and believe that the women keep pulling them back to the outdated, softer and childish ways. Initially they get confused between the paces of the matural and the natural world, but the more they meet the members of their own gender, the more convinced they get about this modus operandi of becoming a winner. They perceive emotional detachment as emotional strength and when combined with their physical strength, it gives them an air of invincibility. They seem to be held in a hypnotic trance where they find bliss in their new-found mantra for success and everything soft looks inferior or frivolous to them. At this stage, if they go unchecked, they run the risk of becoming living examples of men who look at women only as sex objects.

The views and roles of women in society carry no weight with such men, and they target the fairer sex with lust rather than love. And most of the time, all this is kept as a closely guarded secret by such men lest it snatches away any lucrative opportunity from their hands. Such a man never gives an opportunity to a woman in her life to feel like a woman and get into her natural role. This man is not able to appreciate that despite his aloofness if the woman is not detaching herself away from him, then that is most probably because she understands and respects (maybe unconsciously) the natural role assigned to her by Nature and not because she is weak. To him, the second option is the only logical reason whereas the truth is that if women would have adopted this logical conclusion, there might never have been a place called home on Earth. Such men have never been able to understand that the heart has a logic of which logic has no knowledge. The reason behind this logic of the heart is the different nature of commandments set for women by Nature.

Soft and tender feelings have a very important role to play in human life. Without them, neither children can grow up into stable and responsible adults nor old persons can get the level of care that they deserve in their final years. As per the model discussed by us, such feelings are best-taken care of by women under the security of well-meaning men. As already pointed out, the female thought process was designed by Nature to be different from males for a number of reasons and they should get the freedom to work that way. Two of the most important reasons for women to be soft at heart are i) they were the chosen ones to give birth to babies and understand them closely ii) their thought process was meant to be opposite to that of men, which has historically tended more towards logic. By being opposite they were meant to provide strong alogical support (or emotional support) to the man of the house whenever he faced trouble from the logical society. This helps in making the bond between the two rock-solid. Those who realize this, work towards cementing the relationship further while others get embroiled in cribbing on differences, leading to a parting of ways. The fairer sex's approach to love is very similar to that of a child. Both tend to think from the heart. Emotions are a very compulsive force in them for which they may go to any illogical lengths.

An idea of the wonderful finesse for caring that females possess can be had from the legend that Lord Krishna, who was an avatar of Lord Vishnu, took birth as a human only to experience how infinitely loving and caring a mother's love for her child is. I would advise the reader to see all the episodes of the TV serial *Yashomati Maiya ke Nand Lala* to understand this. This level of attachment and devotion cannot be expected from a man. It is just not his forte. For this reason, it is imperative that gender studies become an important part of the syllabus taught to high school children.

After centuries of shackles, women have now started rediscovering themselves. If marriages have to be made successful and wonderful, men also need to rediscover themselves and give women a chance to blossom just like a father gives to his child. It is his emotional support which is important for her to feel at home. Unfortunately, though, the all-prevalent male gaze only sees her sexuality and hardly ever gives her a chance to fulfill her 'natural role'. In fact, most men that we come across today are generally so insecure themselves that sparing a wayward smile for a child on the road itself is a Herculean task for them; so expecting a heart large enough to let a lady bloom is certainly a tall order.

Most men have remained bogged down so much by politics, business, religion, sex or a combination of these factors that their knowledge of the fairer sex can at most be called sketchy. That's why women have been getting a raw deal from them since time unknown till now. They have been torturously cutting these messengers of peace and love to size instead of growing up themselves. And it is the same story with an illiterate rustic of yesteryears as with the metrosexual of our age. As far as gender sensibilities are concerned, we are still living in the Stone Age!

The Two Sexes are Wired Differently

One thing that has become clear from our discussion till now is that the fairer sex loves being supported emotionally. Further, it is common knowledge that children and old people also desperately need and demand emotional support. So, if such a large chunk of the human population needs and desires emotional support, it is a sad revelation of the state of mind of the male youth of today that they consider it unmanly to ask for and give emotional support. There is no denying the fact that the pressure of a logic-driven modern lifestyle on them is very high. However, unless they learn the importance of emotions in human life, they will never be able to give this kind of support which is so important to experience the thrill of being wanted not for money but just for being there. And till the time this does not happen, innocence, love and respect have very bleak chances of survival. So, men should better hurry up before age catches up with them also and they no longer remain in a position to give.

A woman, on the other hand, should justify her 'natural role' by trying to understand her husband from his point of view with the realization that being the opposite gender, his ways of doing the same things will be different. In this way, women can avoid being accused of being hypercritical and, so to say, mothering their husbands. When you continuously criticize somebody and keep on disapproving of his ways, then apart from irritating, in many cases, it takes away the sense of self-respect from the accused and the result is a confrontation. One of the main reasons for the difference of opinion between a man and a woman is that man doesn't like being over-emotional about anything due to his allergy towards emotions, as discussed earlier. What a man would love from his woman is care and faith in his abilities to give her the world of her dreams.

The situation has taken an unexpected turn after girls started getting educated. Traditionally it was believed that women mature early vis-a-vis men because they were able to appreciate the value of love and respect early in life. Now, with women earning at par with men, the overpowering influence of money on their psyche has even broken this age-old belief as stories of women walking out of their homes for living an opulent life are coming to the fore. With money power ruling the roost, the opposite sexes see each other through the lens of power. So, girls today are reluctant to sacrifice their entire life by marrying into a boy's family, who in turn view marriage as a compulsion of the girl's family. The main issue of love is lost on both. They no longer see it as the start of another relationship of love that will bloom to form a new family.

Leaving behind shattered husband and children is no longer an anathema to many modern women. Some instances of women adopting prostitution as a part-time career to live a glamorous life have also been reported.

So, you can well imagine how susceptible a human body is to 'influences.' Therefore, we should be talking about 'enabling' women rather than 'empowering' them because they are also as vulnerable to the toxic effects of power as men. There are reports that by adopting men-like lifestyle, women have also started experiencing adverse health issues like an increase in heart attacks despite the protection that the hormone oestrogen offers them from such attacks. Similarly, instances of uncontrolled anger and impatience are also increasing among women.

Under the blinding influence of money and the accompanying power it is supposed to possess, a majority of men and women today have started viewing their spouses as competitors, leading to a tremendous increase in cases of marital discords. As if the competition at the workplace was not enough, its ominous presence at home has delivered the final blow to intimacy in relationships. Such wrong notions have given rise to most of the maladies found in society today such as adultery, rapes, divorces, murders, etc. Mind you, spouses are not meant for competition. Instead, they are far more than friends. They are, in fact, your natural agents of complete relaxation. And it is entirely up to the honesty in your support to make the other feel like that and spill his/her heart out.

One of the most common problems that teenagers of both sexes face sometime or the other in their formative years is to compulsively feel attracted towards a certain member of the opposite sex and believe that the two of them have been made for each other. They are prepared to go to any extent to save and nurture that relationship. This phenomenon can at best be described as *infatuation* where one's emotions run amok. One should first learn to rein in his/her emotions and then build up a relationship, to avoid making a mess of one's life at a time when Nature is making you mentally and physically capable to enter into a responsible independent relationship.

We have learnt in previous pages that the perspectives of the two sexes in life are very different, so it requires a certain level of maturity to handle these differences. Moreover, appearances are deceptive because external beauty can be bought. It largely depends on money power, and money can be earned through millions of illicit routes. However, inner beauty largely comes through knowledge or faith in goodness or both. So, inner beauty can be trusted as it would hardly ever betray you to harm you seriously. It would at least respect you as a human whereas an externally beautified person generally respects you for your power alone. Infatuation fails to recognize these differences and so mostly ends up in a mess.

The young need to understand that circumstances play a major role in shaping the life of an individual and many a time circumstances are beyond one's control. Sometimes, Nature decides to hit you really hard at the place where it hurts the most, and if you are ill-equipped, you fall off balance and all your commitments and plans for life go for a toss. It makes good sense, therefore, to first equip yourself professionally and emotionally to the best available standards and then take the plunge. 'Falling in love' is easy, but you should first prepare yourself to be able to 'stand in love' also. Hence, in the next chapter, we shall try to understand the general nature of emotions and how they can be controlled.

An ugly offshoot of the fast pace of life that we are living today is impatience. We are never satisfied with the life that we are living. We continuously clamour for more power, more money and more gizmos for our homes. Therefore, we are always rushing, hoping to get eternal peace of mind at some point in this race. What we fail to realize is that the ultimate truth of this rat race for money is that it never ends. Continuous technological innovations keep on pushing your desires further. They ensure that you never rest and are always on the run unless you willfully break away and decide to divert your focus from money to love, as discussed in the second chapter. Impatience generated from this fast pace of life leads to anger, violence and a host of other body illnesses such as high blood pressure, heart attack, stroke, etc. In the next chapter, therefore, we shall also try to learn how to tame anger and, as a consequence, violence. This negative emotion has the potential to abruptly bring to an end many a flowering relationship.

7

Keep Anger on a Tight Leash

Love is one of the most positive and constructive emotions that Nature has blessed humans with. But, Nature has also armed humans with another emotion called Anger, which works exactly in the opposite direction. It is one of the most negative emotions found in the human body amongst many others like greed, disgust, jealousy, hate, etc. Over the centuries, it has contributed to breaking countless love stories and has been the villain behind innumerable incidents of domestic violence and abuse. It has been the reason behind thousands of divorces and broken homes. Hence, it is important to understand the working of this emotion also when we are learning to foster love in relationships.

The First Lady Eleanor Roosevelt of the USA had very aptly said, "Anger is just one letter short of danger." This is true because when you are angry, it is natural that you will do or say something which will hurt the other person, no matter whether it is correct or not. To counter this, the other person will do the same for you, without realizing that two wrongs never make one right. As the cycle progresses, somewhere the missing letter 'D' gets attached to the emotion on display and a dangerous situation evolves. And we all know that nothing good comes out of a dangerous situation. It may lead to the severing of long-standing relationships and violence of the most heinous kind.

Health-wise also, anger can lead to a dangerous situation. Anger can impact the arteries that supply blood to the heart and the electrical system that tells the heart when to beat, and it can affect the heart muscle as well. If you already have conditions that affect the cardiovascular system, moments of anger may leave you more vulnerable…your blood pressure can increase, blood vessels can constrict and inflammatory cells can be released. This can lead to the rupturing of plaque inside a coronary artery… and that can cause a heart attack. Doctors also talk about the gut-brain connection, the link between our emotions and our stomach. Anger can trigger malabsorption of food leading to loss of appetite or cramps.[17]

Since people in today's world are more aware of their rights than ever before, fighting for their rights has become an obsession for many of them. More often than not, this obsession is so deep-seated that such persons have practically become less aware of their duties. Hardly anybody has the time today to think that the majority of the rights are not birthrights. They have to be earned by performing duties. For example, a city won't get smooth traffic on roads unless the citizens themselves obey traffic rules. The right to love also falls in this category.

Usually, we take our close relations for granted and expect a free continuous flow of care and respect from them. Thus, unconsciously we are asking the other person to perform his/her duties while we conveniently keep track of all the rights that we enjoy in that relationship. This behaviour comes very high on the scale of dishonesty since we have stopped reading and attending to the desires of that person. Such lopsided relationships gradually become a load to tow and lose their charm. When rights and duties don't go hand in hand, angry outbursts become the norm rather than the exception.

Let us first try to have a closer look at emotions in general, before studying anger in more detail. Emotions, which are found in such abundance in our body, are like a *bouquet of powers* given by Nature in the hands of each human being. It is up to him/her to use them for the goodwill of self/society or to use them otherwise. And emotions behave exactly like two other mighty powers that we are familiar with in our daily lives viz. Fire and Water. Fire and water are very good servants but terribly bad masters i.e., as long as they are under control, they promote life on Earth by providing living beings with cooked food and drinking water. However, once they become masters, they are capable of bringing about untold destruction of life and property through infernos, wildfires, floods, etc. Hence, like fire and water, emotions should be kept under control and not allowed to master you. Positive emotions should be given more leeway to operate, but negative emotions should be kept on a tight leash as they can lead to very ugly results in relationships and otherwise too.

Since anger is a negative emotion, it is imperative to learn to control it. This can be done by consciously avoiding getting into an ugly situation and when we are into it already, then consciously dragging our attention to a diversion. Forbearance is an important quality that we all need to inculcate by accepting the fact that since variety is the essence of this world, there will always be people whose views will be different or even opposite to ours. Opposite viewpoints are important for maintaining this essence of our world, just as this world needs both Sun and Moon although their behaviour is diametrically opposite.

This world witnesses so much conflict everyday because the opposite of almost everything exists here. Instead of understanding the opposite and following the middle path, we spend a major part of our life correcting the opposite. Opposites or the different viewpoints show us a different way of looking at things. So, instead of outrightly opposing them, try to see the unseen or try to see the already known through a different perspective. Respect the diversity that Nature has blessed us with.

A sure-shot method to avoid an ugly situation at home due to angry outbursts is to learn the art of bending.

There is an old saying in Hindi which goes like this:

Jo jhukte hain unme jaan hoti hai,

Akre rehna murde ki pehchan hoti hai.

This can be loosely translated into English as:

Alive are those, who can bend to give,

Those who can't are like a corpse,

As they have practically ceased to live.

How true! So, learn the art of bending to listen to the views of your partner, in order to let him/her get into his/her natural role. Nature has always rewarded those who learn to bend, as is evident from the fact that only those branches of a tree bear fruits that can bend. Those who can't, either break off and die or spend a lonely colourless life.

Our daily interactions with our partner may involve many unpleasant moments and misunderstandings which may lead to anger. Even a slight slip of the tongue or a wrong tone in your voice can sometimes generate misunderstandings. Sometimes when a bespectacled person is sitting without his specs and doesn't recognize somebody because of blurred vision, his failure to acknowledge the presence of the other person is taken as an offence. So, even a wrong facial expression, whether done intentionally or accidentally, can become a cause of misunderstanding. Such small misunderstandings can be removed easily by the frequent use of 'I am sorry' every now and then. It is important to remember always that it is human to make mistakes and many times the small mistakes that we keep on making become a reason to laugh, which helps in bonding.

However, the most common reason for anger to raise its ugly head in the life of a couple is the misunderstandings arising out of the unidirectional approach adopted by each partner even after they are in a relationship. Without realizing that the two genders think and demand support differently, each of them keeps on giving support in the way they will support a member of their own gender. Thus while you are trying to give your best to save a relationship, things keep on getting worse by the day.

This leads to pent-up feelings and anger. Here comes the need to understand the different needs of the opposite sex and then support him/her accordingly.

In his book *Men are from Mars, Women are from Venus,* John Gray says that one of the biggest differences between men and women is how they cope with stress. Men become increasingly focused and withdrawn while women become increasingly overwhelmed and emotionally involved. He feels better by solving problems while she feels better by talking about problems. Not understanding and accepting these differences creates unnecessary friction in their relationships. The author goes on to explain this by means of a very common example. When Tom (husband) comes home, he wants to relax and unwind by quietly reading the news. He is stressed by the unsolved problems of his day and finds relief through forgetting them. His wife, Mary, also wants to relax from her stressful day. She, however, wants to find relief by talking about the problems of her day. (Their different ways create tension). Tom secretly thinks Mary talks too much, while Mary feels ignored. Without understanding their differences they will grow further apart.

In the last chapter, we attempted to study the different behaviours of the two sexes for this reason only. Gender education, as pointed out earlier too, is very important to bring peace in the lives of young men and women. Till that happens, a very practical way to avoid misunderstandings is to closely study each other's behaviour and talk things out. With your partner, you have to project yourself as vulnerable. When a partner projects himself as powerful, understandings reduce further because people usually submit meekly before power and hide their real selves under a mask. Since it is impossible to become an expert in emotions, you can become a boss in a money-making venture but never in an emotional relationship. In an emotional relationship, it is necessary to find out the real person hiding behind the mask. Therefore, *learn to talk and listen.* Unless you listen, you can never be honest with your partner. When you don't have the time or attitude towards listening, nobody will reveal his/her secrets to you, and where there is no scope for sharing emotional vulnerabilities, love dies slowly and painfully. Listening is, therefore, the key requirement in love. Similarly, unless you talk things out, how on earth do you expect your partner to come to know about your anxieties, worries and desires? Every human being has a different perspective on life, especially the opposite gender. Secretiveness destroys relationships and is an open invitation to anger.

Nature does not provide any of its resources in pure form. It is the man-made science or the man himself who runs after perfection. That is perhaps why they have overvalued 'confidence' so much and distributed degrees to young graduates that proclaim them as 'experts.' Although they might be experts in their own field, they behave as if they are experts in relationships too. Since nobody can be confident in human relations, your only way of doing justice to a relationship is by listening and spending time with that individual in order to understand each other and build up trust. Anger in relationships can be effectively brought down in this manner. If misunderstandings and doubts of each other are regularly rubbed away by the partners through this mechanism, the very fodder on which anger feeds vanishes. This will leave plenty of room for mutual warmth to descend upon the two.

As discussed before, the business world today is bent upon working at such a breakneck speed that they have virtually become slog houses where employees have been reduced to commodities. Everybody here is worried about the competition that the business faces and consequently wants to extract more man-hours from the employees. The management comfortably chooses to ignore the fact that the people who are working to make them meet their goals are humans after all. New medical research has shown that the deadline culture among corporates is assuming deadly proportions by burning out middle and top-level executives very fast. Hence the employees themselves should wake up and realize this, and keep their homes free from the competition of their profession. Since we have learnt that "the home is where the heart is," *the competition must be kept out of the boundaries of home.* At home, it is the reverse that works, i.e., honest support for each other. It is desirable therefore to make your office a place where you get complete professional satisfaction and your home a place where you get complete emotional satisfaction.

I hope that in light of what we have discussed till now, you will help spread the message of love by practicing it yourself first because practicing does not necessarily follow from reading unless it carries with it the requisite effort and conviction. In matters of heart, time alone can judge whether you have the requisite sincerity to carry the responsibility of a relationship into which almost everybody jumps on instinct. Patience is a boon while speed is a curse in relationships. As they say, good things take time but great things take a little longer.

8

Spirituality as an Expression of the Sense of Love

*I*n this age, everybody is rushing from home to the workplace and back. Companies are demanding supernatural levels of energy from their employees. Consequently, the common man has forgotten that relaxation, leisure and spending time with the family are also worthwhile goals as they bring mental peace. Human beings have been reduced to money-minting machines by the corporate world. Competition has been taken literally to cut-throat levels. Business czars have conveniently forgotten that there is lot more to humanity than money.

They know very well that economies need money to remain healthy, but they have blissfully chosen to ignore the fundamental fact that for a human being to remain healthy, emotional fulfillment is as important as professional fulfillment. Money brings power and power commits excesses. Since excess of everything is a deviation from the middle path (the most sensible path of life) and when it is committed at such levels as is being done today, it has a seriously adverse impact on the mind as well as the environment. Spirituality helps in blunting this impact as it infuses in its practitioners a sense of love for the humanity as a whole.

Spirituality refers to the belief in a higher purpose of life, not limited to our sensory experience. It teaches you to focus on oneness of the entire universe, which by the way is what the Big Bang Theory proposed by scientists also implies. Spirituality has helped many to make sense of the seemingly chaotic interconnected world we live in today, as it believes in universal love rather than individual materialistic pursuits. Materialism is driven by belief in the power of money to bring happiness in life while spirituality is driven by belief in a higher form of consciousness to bring peace in life.

Money-driven mentality focuses more on competition and hence speed. It requires huge amounts of energy from you in the shortest possible time. It creates a mirage that money will someday give you a painless world in which there will be no suffering for you. Hence, you get into the habit of overworking yourself to attain that state. However, greed and jealousy never let you attain that state and you remain dissatisfied because of the rising profit level of your competitor or because of your own rising aspirations and expenses. This gives rise to impatience and tension. And this cycle goes on because the moment your efforts start giving results, you again increase your target level. This again leads to increased demands on your body and time. Slowly, the shortage of time starts taking its toll on your emotional well-being and overworking starts taking its toll on your physical well-being. The former shows up in the form of anger and in some cases violence while the latter shows up as diseases like heart attack, high blood pressure, etc. Hence, the end result of such a person can be very pitiable.

As explained in Chapter 1, we all are different expressions of the same infant God who is on Earth to spend his childhood. This childhood is very long compared to any single life. To keep rushing about in life for material benefits takes away the most important experience that defines childhood, i.e., love. Your relentless work for material gains serves only a part of the childhood experience of the infant God. By being materialistic, you black out from your life the other part of the childhood experience which is equally important i.e., the love experience. It is this part that provides the sweet nectar of life. Without love, life loses its natural flow and becomes mechanical.

Money provides a mirage of happiness and without thinking twice we grab at it with all our might as if our existence solely depends on it.

D.H. Lawrence has dealt with this madness for money so beautifully in his poem *Money-Madness*. He says that people are so mad about money that they will force the poor to eat dirt. It is this fear of money-mad fellowmen that everybody is afraid of. At the end of the poem, he exhorts the society to regain sanity about money before we all start killing each other. I would advise the reader to read the full poem to have an idea of the severity of the problem.

Although the poet talks about people in general, the harsh reality is that this madness doesn't respect even close relationships today. (M)oney (O)ften (C)hokes and (K)ills (E)motional (R)elationships of (Y)ore nowadays and makes a MOCKERY of the most positive emotion gifted to us by Nature. To avoid getting into the quicksand of materialism under the hypnotic spell of money, we need to peek into the lives of the great souls of yesteryears. All these great souls, without exception, have advocated keeping humanity as the first priority in all our dealings.

Lord Krishna had beautifully taught this lesson in his famous discourse to Arjuna in the *Bhagavad Gita*. He said that when human values (*Dharma*) are under threat from the egos of the rich and mighty, we must protect these values even if it requires the elimination of those who may be related to us but are evil minded. In this war, which is depicted so explicitly in the great epic *Mahabharata*, the Pandavas killed and defeated the Kauravas although the latter were their cousins and were far more powerful. The scriptures are replete with stories that drive home this point. Today, the world is again forgetting human values under the overwhelming influence of money and power. We are busy killing humanity as fast as we can by destroying our environment without any remorse in the name of progress.

Swamy Vivekananda said, "Like the caterpillar that takes the thread from its own mouth and builds its cocoon and at last finds itself caught inside the cocoon, we have today bound ourselves by our own actions. We have set the wheel in motion and we are being crushed under it."[18] He advocated pursuing spiritual knowledge to get out of this mad spree. He wanted education to teach humans their real nature so that power prevails hand in hand with goodness.

To err is human. The corporates of today conveniently forget the truth underlying this age-old maxim and demand positive results from all your actions. This superhuman demand slowly but surely builds up stress and you end up thoroughly exhausted, both mentally and physically. Just as the owners of these slog houses of today believe firmly in the Darwinian law of 'survival-of-the-fittest', you must also think in terms of the same law but with a difference. A human body remains fittest when it is looked after professionally, physically, emotionally and spiritually. The people who concentrate only on the first two live in a fool's paradise. They realize the truth of this when they reach their professional peak without a healthy state of mind and/or healthy relationships.

So, stop fuelling the rat race further and give your plans to attain material richness a break. Invest some time in becoming spiritually rich as well. A spiritually rich person is by default a caring person. You can contribute a lot to humanization of the modern society in this manner. Governments can also help in bringing about this transformation by making it mandatory for corporates to contribute to a social welfare fund. These contributions can be used for social projects aimed at eradicating poverty, illiteracy and disease from the world so that everybody can live a life of dignity.

Money becomes counterproductive when it starts belittling wisdom and gives power to the hands of immature minds. Such minds become instrumental in bringing a general fall in the standards of education and entertainment in society. A hint of this can be taken from a general fall in the standards of popular films and songs being churned out these days. On shedding emotions and ethics, it becomes very easy to earn money because almost everything sells nowadays. Even contracts to kill their own parents for grabbing their wealth are up for sale! Money brings power and power has its own way of winning all the battles. However, what it can't win are relationships that exude warmth. It is this factor that goodness realizes and understands, and hence stops its lust for money beyond a certain point.

Everybody knows that to earn big money you need a killer instinct but when you start believing in it literally, you don't stop yourself from breaching the point beyond which all ethical and humane restrictions that hinder your pursuit of money are removed. At this point, goodness realizes the futility of moving beyond whereas badness marches on with the brutality of a mad elephant. This is how beasts of the human variety are created because better sense never gets a chance to prevail over them. A word of caution is warranted here for the innocent and uninformed. Human nature is such that when victims of these beasts start hating them intensely, they have every chance of becoming beastly themselves unless they learn to put this negative emotion on a leash. So, beware of intense negative emotions! They have the power to convert you exactly into the person you once loved to hate.

Ancient saints realized the power of spirituality to proliferate goodness in society and also the power of money to corrupt the common man. Hence, they had laid down rules of moral conduct for the common man. For ordinary members of the society, rules of moral behaviour had been laid in such a way that they could blindly follow them without going into details. So, till the time these rules were followed in good faith without questioning, human society did not witness ugly signs of modern life, such as domestic violence, corruption, stress, suicides, etc. at such a large scale. Common people used to be short on money and long on spirituality. Thus, they were largely simple, god-fearing and helpful people who used to participate wholeheartedly in one another's moments of happiness and despair. The effectiveness of these rules can even today be seen in monetarily lower rungs of the society where materialism has not yet made deep inroads. Even the older generation today are living examples of that bygone era.

With the onset of the money-driven industrial revolution, all rules of ancient life seem to have been turned on their head. In the modern world, it is no longer practicable to remain simple. Smartness is the demand of the time we are living in. Consumerism rules our lives and all ugly facets of money are staring us in our faces. However, we can't ignore the fact that money has its nobler side too. It helps empower the weak and gives hope to the unfortunate. That is why it becomes imperative for us to take a closer look at the teachings of our ancient saints in order to ward off the evil effects of money on our behaviour as a society. It will help us know who we truly are and how winds of modernity have blown us away from our true selves. When smartness is sprinkled with the clear water of spiritualism, it washes away the black soot of brashness and shallowness of thought that comes inbuilt into almost all smart human packages available in society today. This paves the way for the light of serenity to percolate into the soul. Spirituality helps in giving meaning to the life that we are living and steers it in the direction in which there is a fulfillment of the soul.

Along with the infinite physical variety in this globally connected matural world comes an equally mind-boggling variety of human intelligence. Spirituality helps us realize that (V)ariety (E)clipses (I)gnorance in (L)ife. When this VEIL of intelligence is lifted, you come to know the infinite ignorance that it had been hiding underneath. Spirituality makes us realize that our collective intelligence is woefully less than our collective ignorance. There is a lot more for us to learn before we can even come close to understanding our universe. This realization brings humility in us and helps us shed our misplaced ego. Can there be a bigger example of our collective ignorance than the fact that after centuries of intelligence-led progress, we are staring at the end of our world? Given the gravity of the scenario we are finding ourselves in today, it would have been far better if we wouldn't have progressed at all!

You will marvel at the fact that it is the same world in which all human beings are living, but everybody views it differently. This is the beauty of this magical path called 'World', created by the greatest magician whom some call God, some call the Supreme Power and some call Nature. Essentially, it is the phenomenon of different influences on different human beings, as pointed out in Chapter 3, that leads to different interpretations of the world by different people. Some people get so awestruck with material richness that they spend their entire lives running after it and don't opt out when they have enough of it. They get addicted to it and keep on inventing new ways to satiate their lust for it.

There are others who get tired of this never-ending rat race and try to find alternative ways available in this world to experience happiness, somewhat like Gautam Buddha. These latter ones are somehow convinced at the back of their mind that this world could not be one-dimensional (money oriented), knowing fully well that the innocence of a child, the unflinching faith of a mother and that lovely look of a woman in love are certainly not things that can be valued by money. Such persons put a check on their materialistic ambitions and slowly open their minds to spirituality because when the interference of money stops, the mind slowly starts providing solutions to questions of love and life.

Thus, spirituality is only meant for persons who want to look at the greater beauty of this magical world. It is not for those who are content with material richness and close all doors to rising to the next level by repeatedly trying to find material solutions to problems that essentially pertain to our innate humaneness. These people don't realize that such problems are the subject matter of a different branch of learning and are outside the realm of money. Lord Krishna had said in his teachings that this world is essentially a *karmabhoomi* i.e., a place where you reap happiness if you work. Similarly, the proverb "work is worship" says work gives us satisfaction, so we should never shirk from work. Even Charles Darwin's theory of 'survival-of-the-fittest' says that those who work and continuously adjust to the changing scenarios in life have better chances of survival.

Those who take these words literally and keep working only in the physical sense of the term 'work' find themselves always engulfed in innumerable problems which generally keep them engaged in finding innumerable solutions to these problems. And thinking that he is a strong believer of these age-old bits of advice, a common man consoles himself time and again that life is like that only, a never-ending ordeal of moving from one problem to the other. But what he has failed to read in these age-old pieces of advice is that 'working' does not necessarily mean 'physical work'. Spiritual enquiry is also work. So, we should work towards removing materialistic *as well as* spiritual scarcity from our lives.

But alas, it is also a fact that spirituality doesn't come easily. Unless a conscious effort is made to probe into it, you can easily miss the bus even though you have all the money in the world to buy the ticket. Today's youth is so much engrossed in empowering itself that it is caught in the whirlpool of money and sex. Money gives it power, and sex, without any strings attached, gives pleasure. This heady concoction leaves him/her with no sense of desire for this third dimension through which dawns the reality of life.

Without this third dimension of spirituality, life looks good and full of thrills for some time only, exactly the way a two-dimensional movie screen takes you into the illusory world full of dreams for a few hours before bringing you back to the real world. Thus, to experience the real bliss of being alive, this third dimension must be explored. More often than not, the third stage of the love cycle kick-starts this journey into the world of spirituality. So, go on, try getting a bit imaginative and join the bandwagon of love to experience this joyful world hidden behind the seemingly impenetrable smokescreen laid by materialism.

Part 2: SWEEET WILL

(S)ave the (W)orld from (E)motional,
(E)nvironmental and (E)conomic (T)rauma by
(W)isdom, (I)magination, (L)ove and (L)ogic

9

Dangers of the Natural World

*M*an invented money to make life easier. However, the main problem with money is that it values the things created or understood by humans only. So, its valuation levels can go only as far as the human understanding levels go. We know that human knowledge (history, science and whatnot) is limited only to a few millennia, whereas life has been here for millions of years. So, money values our knowledge of these few thousand years and conveniently ignores all those years when we were not here but the Earth's ecosystem was very much here, alive and kicking. It assumes that whatever knowledge we have at this moment is the ultimate truth. It has, for example, assumed that we live only once (the famous YOLO approach to life) and so we need to live fast to experience every possible leisure and pleasure that this world has to offer. Nothing can be stupider than this.

The fundamental truth about life on this planet is that it has been existing on this planet for millions of years and will carry on in the future as well. From the various cyclic processes that we observe in Nature like the oxygen cycle, water cycle, nitrogen cycle, the occurrence of day and night as well as the four seasons in a year etc., it is clear that cyclic motion is among Nature's favourite paths of motion. Who knows that science will one day have evidence to show that lives are also similarly recycled in Nature? In fact, many ancient scriptures mention this as gospel truth. Let me share here a fact that I recently came across in *Ripley's Believe It or Not*. It said that philosophers in ancient Greece and India propounded the existence of atoms more than 2000 years before their existence was actually proved by scientists.[19]

So, just because science cannot prove at this point in time that life also gets recycled doesn't mean that it is a wrong assumption. Otherwise also, as Homo sapiens, which in Latin means 'wise man', it is our duty that as we have aspired for a better life for us, our progenies also must enjoy their lives. By usurping all available resources at such a breakneck speed, we are making it more and more difficult for our future generations to enjoy these bounties of nature and live a peaceful life. Also, in Nature, usually, only destructive forces move at high speeds like tsunamis, cyclones, blizzards, coronavirus, etc. No form of life in Nature, moves at such a pace as we aspire to. In Nature, neither time is important nor money, whereas for us 'time is money' is the survival mantra nowadays that keeps us on our toes twenty four by seven. How out of sync are we with our creator? So, we all need to be responsible and slow down in order to use the money for the purpose it was invented by us—to make life easier for us and our future generations.

Every human being has to confront with two opposite facets of life on this planet. The first is the endless time span of Nature and the other is the short life span of living beings. Going by the age of the universe, it is clear that Nature is not under any pressure of time. The rivers have been flowing at their own set pace, the winds have been blowing at their own set pace and living beings have also been growing up at their own set pace since eons. None of these activities of Nature show any signs of hurry because Nature is going to be here forever and for it, there is no urgency of time. On the other hand, the short lifespan of humans compels us to get everything before we die. So, we are always in a hurry. Most of us are able to relate with the latter facet of life more and less with the former in our daily lives.

The main problem with the latter is that we become overly interested in money and get busy creating an artificial, fast-moving and dazzling world (the matural world) around us that is devoid of any love and empathy. However, as pointed out above, the real creator isn't interested in such a fast life. It wants life to live, love and procreate in order to go on and on. Therefore, the only practical solution that is feasible in such a conflicting scenario is to follow the middle path. That is why hybrid humans have chosen the middle path as a way of life.

Due to the blinding speed with which the matural world is working, modern man is now more conversant with the rules of this artificial world rather than the real world created by Nature. The ecosystem of money created by him and his skyrocketing ego have strained or destroyed relationships. So, if he has forgotten his relations even with fellow humans, how can we expect him to think about other species and their contribution towards making the real world? This unbridled power is slowly sinking man deep and deep into his artificial world where only selfishness and power rules. In contrast, however, all species contribute and care for the environment in their own ways in the real world. The quest to take GDP higher and higher is killing the love and care that is the essence of the real world because each species is dependent on others.

Our environment can be compared to Windows, the operating system for computers. The computers wake up and function properly as long as Windows is able to control all the functions. Similarly, we can function properly as long as the necessary operating system, that is, our environment, is working properly. If we act selfishly and don't care about the other species in this environment, the environment will slowly get corrupted and one day life will extinguish, just like a computer stops running when Windows is corrupted. Love for others in our environment is therefore the anti-virus software that is needed to check the virus of selfishness and greed to prevent our operating system from crashing. Maybe that's why the Bible says that the meek shall inherit the Earth because a meek person will need and promote love and care and, hence, contribute to the continuance of the real world. As against this, the powerful will destroy the world because of their ego, selfishness and greed.

The desire to make this world more matural than natural will only accelerate our journey towards our doomsday unless we start acknowledging that we are living in a world built by Nature. We need to realize that Nature has been here for eons and also intends to carry on in the future, with or without us. So, unless we start understanding and respecting Nature, we will continue to make life difficult for us on this planet. Our current knowledge of the universe is, at best, only rudimentary compared to that of Nature. Have we ever stopped for a while in our mad race to reflect that if amassing wealth and knowledge would have been the purpose of life on Earth, then birth and death, the two defining events of any life form, do not make sense as both of them are a hurdle? Amassing wealth or knowledge would have been far easier if all life forms were able to live for ever. Since living forever is not an option for us, it would be better if we become more realistic in our daily pursuits and start aligning ourselves with Nature and its rules as it's already too late. Our situation is like that of a person telling an engineer of a sophisticated car that his own understanding of the car is enough for his daily needs and so he doesn't need him. But, when our car is in dire need of repair and we don't approach the engineer and don't do what he says because of our ego, we can very well end up in a hospital, if not a mortuary.

We can understand our current situation with the help of another example. Nature has made the world and us too, and so, Nature is our mother. Money has, however, been made by man. When we get overly obsessed with money, it is like we are getting busy with our toys. A mother always knows best how to bring up a child lovingly. But if the child gets overly busy with its toys and stops listening to its mother, the mother is bound to get angry after a certain point and discipline the child by punishing him/her. Climate change represents this anger of Nature. It is very soon going to make our life really difficult unless we mend our ways.

Tim Ferris, the life-hacking author and podcast star who was an angel investor in Silicon Valley for a decade, said that many of the super-rich people have been "navigating work and life in sixth gear for decades. Once they have no financial need to work—are 'post-economic'—they have trouble shifting into lower gears." Stevan Berglas, a psychologist and author said, "The rich need greater excess just to feel the same high. If you are an alcoholic, you are going to take one drink, two drinks, five drinks, or six drinks to feel the buzz. Well, when you get a million dollars, you need ten million dollars to feel like a king. Money is an addictive substance."[20]

The time has come for the super-rich of the world to become realistic and de-addict themselves from the fatal attraction of money. They have a great responsibility on their shoulders to slow down the world and save it from impending disaster in the form of climate change.

When money comes easily, people tend to apply shortcuts to get what they want. By applying these shortcuts they are essentially ignoring wisdom in order to make a quick buck. This is because wisdom is always slow to come by as it needs experience. In this world which is rushing all day long for more and more power, it is therefore not in demand. When such shortcut-loving smart people start earning big time, it glorifies mediocrity in society and ultimately leads to the empowerment of such persons who are miles away from understanding Nature and its creations. As a result, real talent takes a beating and is ignored and wasted.

It can be seen today that film celebrities are the highest-paid persons in most parts of the world and the majority of them are dispensing their half-baked wisdom to all and sundry through their films. Instead of valuing doctors, engineers, police and army personnel, etc. who are real heroes, the world today values film heroes the most, even after witnessing the daring real-life heroics of these professionals during the coronavirus pandemic. This is the stage of our collective wisdom today. Giving power into the hands of ignorants/novices can only bring doom. The danger of global warming looming large on us today is due to this misconception of empowering everybody through money. When ignorants get empowered, intelligence and wisdom suffer. In fact, that was the reason why in ancient India, kings used to include sages and wise people in their council of ministers.

How money gives power in the hands of immature progenies of rich by parading them as intelligent and wise has been brought out so well in the following old Punjabi saying:

Jinhan de ghar daane; Ohna de kamale vi sayane

When loosely translated into English, it means, "Even the half-witted children of the rich are treated as wise by the world." In the popular comic series *Graffiti*, I recently came across something similar. It said, "Money talks – It says 'Not Guilty'."[21] Similarly, money talks in other ways also like 'Not failed,' 'Not required,' 'Not necessary,' and so on and so forth. So, excess money power leads to the empowerment of the ineligible, which in turn leads to corruption, ignorance and injustice. We regularly come across the insensitiveness of money-obsessed youth towards the poor in our daily lives.

I remember having coffee in a posh South Delhi market last year when a poor, hungry old woman approached a group of super-rich young boys and girls asking for money or food. This group was having fun and buying expensive snacks just to keep each other company. None of the group members even offered any food item to her even though it was obvious that she was a visibly hungry hapless old lady. This made me wonder how emotionless money power has made us all. We can't see the pain of old also. We desperately need to convert our children back to human beings from the zombies that they have become under the influence of money. If the proverb "excess of everything is bad" is accepted as truth by the world, then why is it not applicable to money? Senator Bernie Sanders once said, "Billionaires should not exist. The wealth disparity in America is a moral and economic outrage."[22]

Money has such an overpowering influence in modern societies that no society has any rule in which excess money is considered bad. That is one of the reasons why the gap between the poor and rich has been steadily increasing.

Usually people run after money to get into a permanent state of happiness but an article in *The Conversation* in 2019 reported that "sustained happiness has no biological basis. A state of contentment is discouraged by Nature because it would lower our guard against possible threats to our survival."[23] Can you now see the mindlessness of our endless addiction to money?

This process of increasing ignorance (or decreasing wisdom) in society with increasing prosperity can be called the *vicious cycle of prosperity*, as depicted in Figure 3 on next page.

As this vicious cycle of prosperity progresses, our tendency to take shortcuts increases because of the power of money that we wield. These shortcuts can be in the form of anger, blackmail, threats, bribes, violence and so on and so forth. The prevalant culture of speed becomes a strong compounding factor for taking shortcuts. Since emotions also are time-consuming and money doesn't like being projected as a loser, it takes another shortcut and forces us into ignoring emotions by thrusting at us the lollypop of monetary gain, again and again. With this, our ignorance of our fellow beings increases further and we understand Nature and its beings lesser and lesser. With emotions out of the way, we give in to greed and show-off more easily, and indulge in an unhealthy competition where the weak and poor are exploited in the name of progress and development.

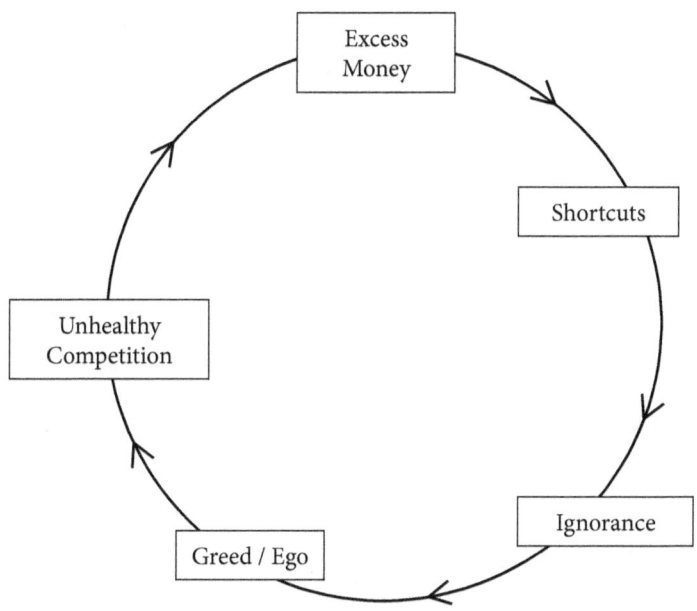

Figure 3: Vicious Cycle Of Prosperity

However, when our understanding of fellow beings decreases, it leads to an increase in loneliness and friction in relationships. The youth today are suffering acutely from the ill effects of this cycle of prosperity. There are reports that loneliness is the latest public health epidemic in the US, costing the health industry billions of dollars annually.[24] This loneliness and friction lead us to more consumerism and/or alcoholism. Increased consumerism in society necessitates more industrial activity leading to a greater carbon footprint for society as a whole. So, this vicious cycle of prosperity is an undesirable phenomenon that must be broken by outside intervention. Love is one such intervention that can break it. Love kills loneliness and friction and promotes care and understanding in society by inculcating the spirit of giving rather than gaining.

It is high time we educated our youth about this power of love and teach them the essence of what Pramukh Swami Maharaj used to say, "In the joy of others lies our own."[25]

The vicious cycle of prosperity perpetuates ignorance and fuels ego. In fact, it shows us how incompetence breeds incompetence in the society which leads to the birth of many other social ills. Women have been suffering because of this cycle since time unknown. Menfolk have hardly understood womenfolk for ages because gender education, even to this date, has been almost non-existent. As a result of this ignorance, the richer and physically more powerful gender kept dictating terms on the softer gender and inflicted misery on them day in and day out. So, this cycle has been contributing to the wastage of lives, talent and resources since time unknown. The government is, therefore, duty-bound to break it. It can do this by making the ultra-rich contribute to social welfare programs aimed at eradicating poverty and promoting a sense of love in the population because economic policies have failed to bring that about. The ultra-rich have managed to manipulate the economy to such an extent that it is now often seen to be widening the gap between the rich and the poor rather than bridging it.

As per the Oxfam International Report 2023 released at the World Economic Forum meeting in Davos, the richest 1% of the world's population increased their wealth by $26 trillion in the past two years. This is twice the increase in wealth of the bottom 99% of the world's population.[26] Most of the rich are now making money just for the sake of making money and this money is simply increasing garbage on the planet and destroying its green resources, both environmental and emotional. A new upgrade of a car or phone series every year are classic examples of wasteful expenditure that is contributing to the increasing garbage on the planet. The money used to produce such needless upgrades that are only filling up pockets of the ultra-rich and destroying green resources of this planet should be immediately diverted by concerted governmental action to the needy sections of society.

When there is so much extra money doing the rounds in this world, is it not a pity that we have brought about a situation where millions of families are suffering the world over due to disease and hunger and millions more are on the verge of suffering extreme hunger and destruction due to climate change related changes. Such monumental economic inequality and the resultant suffering can only be the result of equally monumental foolishness.

The great Urdu poet Ghalib rightly said, "There is no dearth of fools in this world. If you go out searching for one, you will find thousands of them."

Similarly, Einstein observed, "Two things are infinite, the universe and human stupidity, and I am not sure about the former." It would not be wrong to add here that human stupidity is also increasing with time exactly like our universe because we are happily busy creating inhospitable conditions for living beings on Earth in the name of progress and development. By which parameters can unleashing of killer heat waves on unsuspecting simple population in large swathes of land in South Asia be called progress?

Money was initially invented as a way of appreciating and using skills of each other to live and let live. Today, that purpose is lost, rather the dominant attitude today is to hoard as much as you can to wield power, live yourself and let others die! Look at the last sentence of the previous paragraph again if you find this statement too far-fetched. Money becomes a big social problem when it becomes a 'by-hook-or-crook' race, that is, when earning moolah is considered the only goal of life. Then there is no end to that race and it has to end in disease or disaster because goodness generally cannot stoop as low as badness can due to lack of ethics in the latter. The path beyond the ethical barrier is traversed alone by badness and it becomes a sure recipe for an impending disaster.

The scenario really takes an ugly turn when persons with ill-gotten wealth become leaders.

The political landscape today can provide innumerable examples of this scenario, where finding a statesman has become as difficult as picking a needle in a haystack. That's why to focus on GDP alone is a misconceived notion, as it gives momentum to the vicious cycle of prosperity further and leads to the creation of a rudderless society where humanity takes a beating and money becomes God. Among those to question the GDP metric was Robert Kennedy, in an eloquent speech in 1968.

He said, "Our Gross National Product is over 800 billion dollars a year, but that Gross National Product—if we judge the United States of America by that—that Gross National Product counts air pollution and cigarette advertising, and ambulances to clear our highways of carnage. It counts special locks for our doors and the jails for the people who break them. It counts the destruction of the redwood and the loss of our natural wonder in the chaotic sprawl. It counts napalm and counts nuclear warheads and armoured cars for the police to fight the riots in our cities. It counts Whitman's rifle and Speck's knife, and the television programmes which glorify violence in order to sell toys to our children."

Thereafter, there was sheer poetry: "Yet the Gross National Product does not allow for the health of our children, the quality of their education or the joy of their play. It does not include the beauty of our poetry or the strength of our marriages, the intelligence of our public debate or the integrity of our public officials. It measures neither our wit nor our courage, neither our wisdom nor our learning, neither our compassion nor our devotion to our country, it measures everything in short, except that which makes life worthwhile. And it can tell us everything about America except why we are proud that we are Americans."[27]

Proper channelization of money is very important and that should be the prime objective of the government. GDP measures the value of the domestic products and services produced in a country during a given period. It is believed that more products and job opportunities lead to more money and hence, less poverty. And since poverty alleviation brings health and happiness, it is a goal worth pursuing. But when poverty has been alleviated, what brings happiness? It is money *and* love. Love is like a domestic service that is a must for bringing happiness. But is that being measured today? No. This is the root cause of increasing unhappiness amongst the middle class and the rich. The giving attitude that is the backbone of love has been dismissed as nonsense by this so-called educated section of society.

German psychoanalyst Eric Fromm expanded the idea of love from a romantic context to a social context. He said that individual love and social love are intertwined and we must learn to love our society with equal humility, faith, courage and discipline. He called this notion of love an "informed art of living that needs to be cultivated over and above money, success, power and prestige which we are all conditioned to pursue."[28]

The rich need to accept the reality that today loneliness and diseases of excess (like obesity, diabetes, etc.) are killing more people than hunger and war. So, the government and the rich should realize that GDP must be adjusted with the value of this service (love for society) to measure *humane progress* rather than progress in the production of commercial goods and services alone. It is this long over-due correction that is required to break the vicious cycle of poverty as well as prosperity. Charity can play an important role to bring this about in cases where the economy has failed miserably to free people from the clutches of poverty. We can take a cue from the advice that the Nobel Prize-winning economist, Abhijit Banerjee, gave to the Indian National Congress (a political party in India) when he suggested donating Rs 2,500 p.m. to the poor in order to pull them out of extreme poverty.[29]

Here, it would also not be out of place to mention that the world can learn a lot from Sikhs when it comes to charitable work. Sikhs have been consistently advocating the spirit of sharing food and other resources with the needy. They have been distributing free food (*langar*) through community kitchens at their *Gurudwaras* for centuries. In recent times, the world saw them distributing free food, medicines, blankets, etc. when they were amongst the first to reach coronavirus victims, victims of war in Ukraine, etc. The government should similarly goad industry to heavily invest in programs aimed at poverty and illiteracy alleviation. GDP should then be calculated after adjusting for such domestic social welfare programs implemented by the industry.

As already discussed, unbridled affluence promotes mediocrity and immaturity in humans. It tends to make everything available easily, which is contrary to the human nature that comes from our basic hunter-gatherer body make-up. A hunter-gatherer experienced real pain in earning a living and hence could easily relate to love as an antidote to that pain. The depth required to understand the real nature of another human being has therefore become more difficult in today's matural world. Money culture has made loving that much harder.

West seems to have taken the Darwinian mantra of 'survival-of-the-fittest' a bit too seriously and in the process made living synonymous with unending competition. However, life doesn't subscribe to this rule so seriously. Nature has intended life to relax, love and enjoy too. To kill innocence/love while pursuing unnatural goals is criminal. If innocence/love were so unworthy goals, why didn't they die out as per the 'survival-of-the-fittest' theory?' Why is Nature not killing innocence/love although we have been discarding them since long in our overenthusiasm for competition? Human beings do not need to be competing and rushing always to survive. This hyperactivity has today brought the world to such a stage where global warming is threatening to destroy the very world in which humans have been competing to survive! Can you see the immaturity of it all? In our overenthusiasm to keep preparing to fight an imaginary enemy for survival, we have actually created such a big monster that will eat the whole world up!

Another example of immature behaviour that we witness today is the culture of nuclear families. A nuclear family is good for the economy because it generates more demand for housing, furniture and innumerable other consumer items, as compared to a joint family. So, for the sake of prosperity, we sacrificed the joint family culture. However, in a nuclear family, the biggest sufferers are the children and the old people. For this, we today prefer expensive options like setting up old-age homes and crèches rather than going back to having joint families. A joint family provides an excellent environment to overcome these sufferings through an in-house balm of love and wisdom, with loads of cost-cutting to boot.

It's a myth that when man-made currency reduces, it leads to the break up of the joint family. In such times, there is a need to increase God's currency, which is love.

This is the cheapest way to overcome difficult times and it only makes the bond stronger. Love can be referred to as God's currency in the sense that it makes us work for others and, in return, makes us feel secure, which are incidentally two important features of a man-made currency also. A joint family is the best place to learn the use of this currency due to the presence of innocence and wisdom in close proximity to each other.

When you raise your standard of living, your cost of living goes up. As a result, if you don't pace up your life, you won't be able to meet the increasing cost. When you pace up your life, the stress won't let you relax adequately and you won't think of increasing your family. So, the married will not think of having more children and the bachelors will not think of getting married. All this because of your love for a better life! The fear of increased cost of living has led the West to decrease population, not cost. On the other hand, the East has increased its population but kept its costs low by not indulging in unnatural lifestyles.

The West has in the process raised its standards of living but at the same time contributed more to the release of deadly global warming gases. The East, on the other hand, has accepted hardship as a way of life and desisted from adopting super-fast industrialization. As a result, they have not been able to kick poverty out of their life but still value emotions and relationships. There is an urgent need today for both lifestyles to merge. This will enable the world to pursue a sustainable middle path where the populace can earn good money as well as adopt a slower lifestyle. It will ensure that poverty is removed from the lives of all and, at the same time, it will bring happiness through increased warmth in relationships.

Remember what Mahatma Gandhi had said: "There's enough in this world for everybody's need but not for everybody's greed." So, there is really no need to panic about adopting a humbler lifestyle.

Human beings have a lot of ills inbuilt in them like they are aggressive, revengeful, greedy, violent, make fun of others and so on. All this troubled human society a lot initially and many of us searched for a solution to make us more civilized and reliable. This led to the development of education. It was believed that it was a sure shot way to make us more tolerant of each other and hence it would ultimately make us live a long meaningful life. But eventually, as the GDP became God, we started putting money before everything else, even education. Soon schools came up that only taught how to promote businesses so that more and more money could be generated. Slowly, money started making inroads into education to such an extent that degrees are literally being bought with money in so many private colleges today.

With this, the very purpose of civilizing human beings by way of education stands defeated! So, people are now back to their devious ways with more power in immature hands. And, as a result, the rich are becoming richer and the poor are becoming poorer. We are now at such a stage of ignorance, rather stupidity, where we are working day and night just for the sake of earning more and more money. Although we are creating conditions for the end of Earth and ourselves, nobody is worried. We are all happily busy with our senseless game of making money. Today, Homo sapiens is behaving like a bully in the class of Nature, where he wants to rule without following the rules of the class.

Science and technology have no doubt helped humans overcome their hardships by providing them with a variety of consumer products and machines. This however is not the best way out because creating more and more consumer products and machines to address various concerns of humans will only enhance global warming. Also, too much dependence on these products and machines is making us lonelier day by day and to overcome it we are seeking respite in liquor, drugs, abnormal work schedules and so on. A better way would be to learn the science behind love also to sort out these concerns of humans and instill in them a sense of love along with that of competition. Since Nature is not depriving our progenies of emotions, ignoring emotions and focusing only on technology to solve our problems will disturb the delicate balance in Nature.

The sheer number and variety of human-made products available today has left us with no time to think about the things that are not valued by humans but are valued by Nature, the creator of humans. By following the middle path, as humans will start realizing the importance of more and more natural bounties that are vital for survival, like love and compassion, money will also start valuing them. Then charity and humanity-driven projects will no longer be looked down upon as undesirable loss-making ventures. This change in lifestyle can come about only through right education. The sooner humans realize the importance of love, the source and sustainer of all kinds of life on Earth, the lesser will be the hardship faced by the present and future generations. Sacrificing their present for a better life for their children comes naturally to parents. Inculcating the same spirit of sacrifice for future generations among today's youth is the need of the hour. They can start by working to uplift the deprived sections of society first just like any parent would provide first and foremost for the most deprived of his/her children.

10

Align With the Natural World

> *"The more clearly we can focus our attention on the wonders and realities of the universe, the less taste we shall have for destruction."*
>
> *– Rachel Carson*

Today, we all are so busy in our race for money that we conveniently ignore this giant automated system called our environment. This automated system is made up of a complicated web of interlinks among different organisms that are themselves made up of even more complicated systems of body, mind and emotions. This system is so intricate yet so efficiently functioning for millions of years that one cannot help but marvel at its beauty! However, we do not value this huge automated system and run after small human-made automated systems like a factory, a car, a rocket and so on. We keep destroying vital parts of the natural system in our mad race to acquire these human-made automated toys. Instead of respecting this wonder of wonders and trying to understand it, we choose to ignore it and get busy following our own small money-led motives. Some are so blinded by their ego that they go to the extent of calling themselves atheists and turn a blind eye to the working of this gigantic machine called Nature.

Let us try to answer one basic question first. Is Nature bigger, wiser and more powerful than man-made industry or vice-versa? This will help us decide that, in the case of conflict between the two, whose say should prevail? To answer this, let us start by answering an even more basic question i.e., has Nature given us our life or the industry? Since we exist because of Nature and the industry exists because of us, Nature is of course far bigger than us and the industry.

The scriptures have been advocating since ages that we have to get rid of 'me' and 'mine' from our psyche. There are very logical reasons behind this advice. Giving undue importance to 'me' vis-à-vis Nature doesn't make sense because even our own body is not made by us, and giving undue importance to 'mine' also doesn't make sense because even the planet we use for living and leisure is not made by us, leave alone our other possessions. All living beings on this planet have been created by Nature and all material things that we call our own have been prepared by industry from the raw materials provided by Nature. Then, is there any justification for 'me' and 'mine', except mindless greed? Keeping industry on a higher pedestal than Nature is another big example of extreme ignorance in this self-obsessed edition of Homo sapiens today.

Human-made things will never be able to bring lasting happiness to us because we humans are creations of Nature and therefore only natural antidotes to life stress can bring lasting happiness. So, learn to respect innocence and love because these two are those natural antidotes. After money has trashed innocence for the hundreds of years that it has been in existence, has Nature stopped producing innocence or has innocence become extinct? The fact that Nature is not incorporating changes brought in by technology in the last 500 years or so in its new progenies clearly shows that Nature is not as excited by our scientific inventions as we are. Babies are still born innocent with not even a trace of money and technology-induced changes evident in them.

Even if Nature incorporates these changes as per the 'survival-of-the-fittest' theory, it will do it at least thousands of years from now. So, to live our short lives happily, it is we who will have to mend our ways according to Nature and not vice versa. Nature has fixed the time period for producing human babies as 9 months since ages and their period of childhood and adolescence is also fixed. Similarly, Earth and other planets have been revolving around Sun in their fixed time periods for millions of years. Nature has never tried hurrying up by experimenting with some new technology during this long period. So let's also slow down a bit and incorporate love into our lives to help build a more Nature-aligned society.

Look at the different life stages of any animal. Life was designed to move at a slow pace, otherwise, long fun-filled years of childhood and youth do not make any sense. Nature could have cut down these slow years and added them to the fast-moving adulthood years. Also, there is a certain speed of life that the environment can tolerate. Beyond this critical speed, the environment starts getting polluted with so much trash that it is unable to dispose of it by itself. So, a certain critical speed of life is essential to sustain life as well as the environment. *Love helps in maintaining that critical range of pace in life by keeping a check on our propensity to speed up.* An individual, his/her emotions and environment are all related to each other.

A basic ingredient of love is care. And if you care, you have to move cautiously. There are so many factors that you have to think of when you love your family. The different members of your family might belong to different age groups and hence their demands might conflict with each other. So, you have to think carefully and spend time with each of them to reach a consensus. A decision taken in a hurry would be good for some and rude for others. The same holds true for the environment. You have to slow down and spend time to understand it. Love and compassion act like speed breakers and help us maintain that critical speed by teaching us the value of caring and giving, and the amount of time that these actions need to really sink in and have the desired effect.

Indian Vedas have long propounded the theory of *Vasudhaiva Kutumbakam* (the whole world is one large family) for this reason. It helps in promoting love amongst humans and also preserves the environment. It is time for the world to adopt love as a way of life and treat the whole world, including the flora and fauna, as one large family. The lifestyle change that everybody should be talking about now is to stop the self-destructive blind run after money and give positive emotions a chance to slow down and cool down the world.

We are today running away from the natural way of living and adopting more and more matural lifestyles because of the comfort that the latter offers. But, have we ever spared a thought about the benefits that a natural lifestyle can bring? The biggest benefit is that it teaches us humility. The life designed by Nature is, no doubt, difficult in comparison to matural lifestyle because it has created this environment common for an infinite variety of life forms. Some things that are good for some animals are bad or fatal for others. A peacock eats poisonous snakes, so in order to have peacocks in this world, Nature had to provide for snakes and lizards too, even though they are poisonous to some other animals including humans. And since lizards feed on mosquitoes, there was a need to have mosquitoes too. Mosquitoes provide life to lizards but are an infinite source of nuisance for humans.

So, in this long chain of interdependence, there are bound to be many irritants. In this complex web of life forms, it is a stupidity to expect life to be a cakewalk. But, we humans think that by using technology, we shall be able to build an all-goody life for us one day that would be free from all such irritants. A question worth pondering here is whether man can ever make machines better than Nature, given his extremely short life span. For example, can man ever beat the factories of Nature, that is, trees that can be grown just anywhere with a seed? As if that was not enough, the products of these Nature-made factories do not display an expiry date but tend to self-destruct when they come close to expiry.

As another example, observe that Nature has created so many living organisms with such complex wiring inside each of them but has not cared to put any kind of value tag on any of them. It has made death also so commonplace. So, in a way making a living being is not a big deal for it. On the other hand, we have made a few complex robots that can perform some rudimentary functions as compared to a living being and we have placed such heavy price tags on them. Their destruction is unthinkable for us! Aren't these two examples alone enough to show the shallowness of the tall claims that we repeatedly make every now and then about our new scientific inventions? Clearly, Nature is far more intelligent and smarter than all of us combined. In fact, it is eons ahead of us. So, we must realize that it must have kept adversity as a part of life for a good reason. Adversity brings us closer to Nature and helps us in having a holistic and more humane worldview. Therefore, it would be better if we learn to acknowledge the greatness of Nature with humility and respect it and its ways before it is too late and lethal heat waves generated by climate change start roasting us alive.

Behavioral history over centuries tells us that men and women are so different in their mental makeup that neither sex can understand the other completely in a lifetime. This is because, over thousands of years of existence, they have evolved different life patterns depending on their own sets of strengths and weaknesses. For example, research studies have shown that generally men have more aggressive and violent tendencies compared to women. Similarly, it has also been documented that women are generally more resistant to hunger, fatigue and disease compared to men.[30] So, many actions that will be automatically understood by a member of the same gender might be understood by a member of the opposite gender after years of observation. As already mentioned in Chapter 1, John Gray has written a whole book on this aspect. When it is so difficult to understand the opposite sex of the same species, it would obviously be much harder to understand our environment, which comprises within it so many species.

When there is so much to understand, speed can only kill. So, when humans speed up due to their higher cognitive power, they obviously do it at the cost of other species in the environment. The numbers of so many other species in the environment are, therefore, continuously dwindling. From the time computers have made their entry into our lives, the race for speed has gone to another level altogether. Modern computer scientists never tire of crying themselves hoarse about the exponential increase in computing space and speed that they have achieved in the last few decades. They need to be reminded that the speed with which they are busily expanding the digital space is peanuts when compared to the speed with which the universe is expanding its physical space!

It is high time we accepted that even though Nature had the capability of bestowing us with speeds close to that of light or radio waves, it opted for a slow life for living beings. Therefore, we have no business interfering with this basic design that Nature, in its wisdom, has set for life. If we still don't mend our ways, we may, in our ignorance, end up destroying this beautiful planet and killing ourselves. All symbols of power and speed in our modern world, whether it is rocket power, atomic power or computing power are like bouquets bequeathed in the hands of the infant God, similar to fire, water and emotions, as discussed in Chapter 7. They are very good servants but very bad masters. When handled with anger, hate or greed, they will bring untold destruction. However, if handled with love and care, they can serve humanity to no end.

This generation might get a thrill from the power generated by speed but they are actually preparing ground to kill the future generations due to the extreme environmental degradation that their actions are triggering. Speed is a sure sign of immaturity and we should avoid it at all costs, especially at this point of time in history when we are literally staring at a holocaust due to our speed mania of the last few centuries. The unprecedented levels of fossil fuel consumption in these centuries are already causing several glaciers to melt leading to rising sea levels all over the world. Its disastrous effects are being witnessed the world over in the form of increased incidents of floods, cyclones, wild fires, earthquakes, etc. And these effects will continue to become deadlier by the day unless we rid ourselves of this fatal attraction of speed. There are so many proverbs in the East and West that discourage speed.

For example:

East: a) *Dheere dheere re manna, dheere subkuch hoye*
Mali seenche sau ghada, ritu aaye phull hoye
(Loose translation: Everything happens slowly in this world. Even if a gardener gives water equivalent to 100 pitchers to a tree, the fruit will grow only when the right season comes.)
b) *Jaldi ka kaam shaitan ka*
(Loose translation: Only people with ill will work with speed.)

West: a) Slow and steady wins the race.
b) Speed thrills but kills.

The time has come to pay heed to the wisdom of these proverbs because the population today is at an all-time high and if so many people are working at full speed, the stress on the environment is bound to increase astronomically. (Just think, so many ignorant people working at full speed!) Slowing down will slow down the destruction of natural resources, accumulation of unmanageable waste, extinction of species, rising of temperatures, etc. which will substantially help in reversing climate change.

We have discussed above that life was designed by Nature to be hard and slow to make us live and love. Emotions help a lot in maintaining such a lifestyle because they are really hard to understand and require time to sink in. Let us suppose that the police catch a murderer red-handed from the murder site. Now, this murderer might be a criminal in the eyes of a police officer but for his mother, he might be a victim who, in a moment of uncontrolled anger, killed his tormentor! Remember, the heart has a logic, of which logic has no knowledge. Even the same spoken or written sentence can be interpreted differently by different age groups and different sexes because the emotions involved are not often captured correctly in words. So, emotional relationships need time to understand, and therefore, there is no scope for speed in emotional relationships. This is, however, a major reason for the generation that swears by speed to ignore them and follow greener pastures.

Another example highlighting the complexity of emotions can be taken from the book *The Kite Runner*, written by Khaled Hosseini. At one point in the story, the rich kid Amir was angry with himself that he couldn't save his friend Hassan (son of a servant in their home) from the torture of Aseef (a spoilt brat), but instead of comforting Hassan, he started ignoring Hassan and even asked his father Baba to oust him along with his father from their house! How illogical is that! But that is how it is with emotions. It has been often observed that highly emotional people not only love intensely but also tend to pick up a fight with their loved ones with equal intensity, that is, their outward actions might sometimes be exactly opposite to their inner feelings. We see again that emotions need time to be understood correctly. This complexity of emotions is also one of the main reasons that has led men to ignore the emotional intelligence of women and instead concentrate largely on their physical beauty. Gender education can help immensely in overcoming this problem.

Science has also been guilty of narrowing down the view of life in humans to physical things. It hasn't focused on emotions due to which relations have become very fragile nowadays. This might have happened because science has been mostly sponsored by the military and capitalism. Due to over-attachment to consumer items and technology that science has introduced us to, people have drifted away from Nature and its not-so-simple-to-understand infrastructure. We have ignored the fact that emotions make this world a happening place by creating so many situations that make infinite human interactions possible. They introduce individuality in otherwise physically similar humans because they are honed by an individual's personal life experiences. As a result, the same ideas sink in differently in different persons. Some people may love doing something while others may find the same act bad or even revolting.

For example, some people may love eating pork or beef but many others would hate it because of the beliefs on which they have been brought up. Emotions make us feel good or bad. Similarly, they make us feel happy or sad.

So, emotions give rise to a variety of situations in life. If life is a play (as per Shakespeare), then emotions are the lifeblood of that play. In fact, these emotions make us human. Using them correctly can move mountains whereas using them wrongly can be equally disastrous, as discussed in Chapter 7. Just because science has ignored emotions doesn't mean that they don't exist or they are useless. Emotions are mostly individualistic in nature while science is more general in nature. So, it is not easy to make general laws for emotions as is done in science today. When science will evolve to study the highly advanced emotional software in living beings, then wisdom will be respected more than money.

Somebody has very rightly said that when you feel directionless, the best way out is to seek guidance from Nature itself. So, in this age, when it has become a trend to be cool about everything including close relationships, let us take a look at Nature to find whether complete freedom in human relationships is a desirable concept. The family of our solar system comprises eight planets revolving around Sun. This relationship of the planets with Sun is surviving only because they are held together by a bonding force called gravitational pull.

This pull is such that it gives enough space to individual planets to move in their independent paths but it doesn't let go of them completely so that every planet can bask in the sunshine. Similarly, relationships of the close kind should also be maintained consciously in such a manner that they provide enough warmth to enable you to bask in the bond. It might make good business sense to be cool about relationships but in matters of heart, it is far more important to radiate warmth.

So, we can learn a lot from Nature because it has perfected a lot of things over the centuries. Similarly it is always wise to respect elders in a society because they can teach you a lot more about the mysteries and realities of life than any number of degrees put together. They have been through life's day-to-day experiences so many times, albeit in a different age, that ignoring their opinions would be tantamount to wasting time and energy to reinvent the wheel.

They might not have kept pace with the new inventions of the materialistic kind but nobody can question the fact that they have a better grasp on the other important constant of life viz. emotions. So, they might have a lower IQ (Intelligence Quotient) but their EQ (Emotional Quotient) and SQ (Spiritual Quotient) would certainly be high. It is not for nothing that there is a saying, "Young people *think* that old people are fools but old people *know* that young people are fools."

The seers of yesteryears used to meditate for long in jungles to understand life and the proper way to live it. As a consequence, they arrived at a certain set of rules for the survival of humans and the environment. These seers were actually service engineers of the most complex automated machine we know of, called the environment. This machine is far more difficult to understand than non-living machines that we seek to understand in engineering sciences. In fact, engineering sciences are child's play when compared to the complexity of the mental and emotional build-up of a human and its convoluted connection with our environment. That is why today college students become experts in their subjects in 4 or 5 years while the seers used to meditate for decades together in the peaceful environs of deep jungles to understand the fundamental questions of life.

And what seers found was no less than a miracle. In those early days when violence and brutality were ruling human societies, they invented religion and how it worked! The majority became religious and started following religious practices. This would have been possible only if the majority would have found peace through their teachings. However, with time, when money started making inroads into religion, religion started getting a bad name, and in modern times, it is looked upon as an affront by the educated majority.

These seers realized the power and complexity of emotions in human life and found that the only school where emotions can be learnt in the right perspective is a joint family where persons of all ages experience joy and pain together. They learn that without pain and nursing the pain, the joy is also fake and short-lived. Love grows manifold in adversity. So, the seers advocated family life for humans (*Grihastha Ashram*), right from micro to macro level. At the macro level, they proposed the theory of *Vasudhaiva Kutumbakam* as mentioned before. The seers strongly believed that we all had an element of God in us but it has to be unlocked gradually by living in harmony. They knew that it takes time to explore the infinite mind space, in fact years and years of discipline and concentration to understand the inner self.

So, they promoted a slow love-filled life rather than a high-speed technological life. While laying out these rules, they knew it would be hard for the youth to understand them due to lack of experience, so they just asked them to follow them blindly as rules under the garb of tradition. These rules of life were followed by the youth as a matter of faith in the olden days and there was respect for elders who had experienced it all and found the experience rich and rewarding. Then money came with its blinding ego and speed and it upset the apple cart. As a result, now elders live in shelter homes, children in creches and the young live with diseases of body and mind. And as if that was not enough, it created such a big environmental mess for which the entire planet will be paying through the nose. The scientific spirit is so far untouched by the realm of spirituality and so traditions are today being challenged by the young but the old still find wisdom in them. Science and spirituality need to go hand in hand for the survival of life and the environment.

Money removes the reason for interacting with others emotionally by removing hunger and insecurity. You start feeling so secure with money that you stop listening to others and speed up to achieve your own personal goals. That is why excess money often leads to deterioration of emotional bonds. This sense of security and achievement that money power seems to provide is the driving force behind this blind race for money and a dramatic fall in EQ of the public at large. Money has made us forget our basic human nature that has developed over centuries over long periods of adversity and poverty. The connection between love and paucity has been expressed so well in the following paragraph taken from a popular Hindi song penned by Majrooh Sultanpuri:

Amiri hai Sitara, Garibi hai ik aansoo

Yeh aansoo hai mohabbat

Mohabbat zindagi hai, Bas itna jaan le tu

When loosely translated into English, it means, "Although prosperity shines like a star and poverty is like a tear dropped from a crying eye, the truth is that the tear evokes love and love is life." So, to experience love again, give the mad race for money a break!

Emotional distress, nowadays, is causing divorces, depression, suicides, alcohol and drug abuse, and so on. The scale at which this is happening now is so large that it cannot be ignored any further. So, why are we not addressing emotional issues? Simply because emotions don't earn us money. Is money really so important in this world where approximately three-fourths of the population (children, women and old) is highly emotional? Because of their innocence or love for innocence, they have been sucked by so-called intelligent people into a system that is madly working towards generating money. This system is killing innocence and love. There is too much cacophony around us, thanks to the power that money has placed in the hands of ignorant people. It's time to rise above this din and get back to the basics to reset our life directions. Women should join forces like never before to buck this trend of neglecting and hence killing innocence, and reinstate respect for innocence and love in human society. This will immensely help in slowing down the world and prevent nihilists from making Earth a planet sans humans.

According to a recent newspaper report, after the advent of AI (Artificial Intelligence), serious discussions are taking place in the scientific community on having a sustainable future without humans![31] Can anything be crazier than this? Yuval Noah Harari has also raised concerns about this prospect in his book *Homo Deus, A Brief History of Tomorrow*. This madness clearly betrays the acute emotional and spiritual bankruptcy of these so-called powerful elites of the world. Gross overuse of intelligence with zero knowledge of the power of love has sickened them so much that they have literally become merchants of death.

Osho rightly said, "The real problem is not the use of too much intelligence but the non-use of emotion. Emotion is completely disregarded in our civilization, so the balance is lost and a lopsided personality develops."[32] This imbalanced group of scientists, politicians and so-called thinkers are in desperate need of awakening their souls to the beautiful world of God all around them in the form of love and innocence. In fact, with AI being increasingly seen as a potential threat to the existence of humans themselves, love education has become necessary as a survival strategy, not only to counter the traditional villains of humankind like loneliness and depression but also to save human society from the massive monsters that are shaping up in the form of climate change and the destructive potential of AI.

In his article 'AI and the future of work' , Arnab Bhattacharya, professor in the department of computer science at IIT, Kanpur writes, "At their heart, all AI models are mathematical tools, albeit too complex for humans to explain. Therefore, anything that can be 'measured' in terms of numbers can be solved by AI models. Thus, humans may not be required for these so-called 'left-brain' functions. This disruption calls for a massive re-skilling of the human population. Humans should now focus on developing and utilizing 'right-brain' skills, such as critical thinking, creativity, emotional intelligence and empathy. These skills are difficult for AI to replicate and will become increasingly valuable in the future of work."[33]

Look at the history of the human race. It's full of battles, wars, deceit and murder. Over the years, however, with an increased understanding of human nature, violent history has given way to more inclusive and caring democracies. But this has happened over a long period of time when the world has spent time to find out the real will of people. Time is, therefore, important for understanding human yearnings. Any speeding up of things due to money power or any other power is against our real human nature. But when we are too involved in the cesspool of power and greed, we hardly spend any time introspecting on this aspect. There are so many unprincipled and immature people amongst us who drag us into this speed mania forcefully or by creating fear. They want to grab power by hook or crook and then make the lives of the wise and the weak miserable by ruling over them. Make no mistake, such elements will always be there. But humanity will have to devise ways to keep such elements in check.

In such a scenario, it becomes incumbent on the civilized human race to give love a chance to propagate and relieve this world from this age-old scourge of mindless profiteering, violence and treachery, especially now when the world is sitting on a mountain of wealth and therefore can afford to bring about these changes. The best way to do this is to adopt the most sensible path of life, i.e., the middle path, proposed by none other than the Buddha. To follow this path, half of the adult population must be totally devoted to the cause of love. And it goes without saying that females broadly represent this fifty percent of the population, not only because they understand emotions better but also because they understand children, the future of this world, better. While following the middle path in this manner, both men and women will be guided by their inbuilt opposite nature which will ensure that neither follows an extreme path.

Women grow up to be mothers and mothers are the ultimate embodiment of love and care for their children. Still, we are nowadays hell-bent on pushing women into the fields that require very harsh physical conditions, like combat roles in Army. We need to understand that a woman will always have to work against her basic nature when she works in such a ruthless power demanding role. Biology tells us that men have more muscle mass while women have more fat in their bodies. So, a woman would always be at a disadvantage when compared to the efforts that a comparable man would require in such fields. And it would be exactly the opposite in a field where love and care are top requirements. Men would be at a clear disadvantage in such fields.

So, it would be far more fruitful if the two sexes live the way Nature has designed them and follow the middle path. Governments should, therefore, work towards a more just society in which women have an equal participation in nation building but the division of work in every field should be aligned with natural roles of each gender. And there should be recognition of the importance of work put in by women by ensuring pay parity. Such an arrangement will throw up many new employment opportunities and at the same time reduce competition between the sexes. I think the most urgent task that women must be entrusted with in all fields is to frame and implement policies that heal the modern societies by freeing them from the clutches of the highly stressful work environments. It will be a yeoman service to humanity. As discussed in Chapter 3, the world today is still so brutal that even young, smart and educated women find it very difficult to work comfortably in a field of their choice. The world desperately needs today a 'Home-Improvement Committee', if I were to use the expression coined by John Gray in the context of the human society as a whole. It should be the endeavour of governments to provide a secure environment to women so that they can carry out their good work without fear.

Women need to urgently get into their natural role of nurturing and caring as it's already too late. They have a huge responsibility of saving future generations from the ill effects of money-addiction. For this, an equal participation of women in government is a must. But, if we go by the current data on participation of women in public life, it seems very difficult to achieve this change in the near future unless an all out effort is made by governments worldwide. Gender education can become a very important tool in bringing about this change.

Females, being birth-givers, are architects of the human body. This could be one reason why they understand advanced human traits like emotions better. On the other hand, men are not so well-versed in these traits. The outside world which was being dealt with by only men till recently consists of different cultures, different age brackets, different mindsets and different species. It is very difficult to understand so much variety in a lifetime. As a result, when men were dealing with different environments and different mindsets till now, they largely dealt with it logically or violently to earn their living. This is because when such interactions happen and there is a lack of knowledge of love, you can either win by brain or brawn.

With some knowledge of love, these interactions can become less cut-throat and more civilized. We just need to understand our different ways of living life in order to reach a common understanding of the most sustainable way beneficial to all. Every living being responds to love positively if only we can build the trust required for it. Women have a big responsibility in bringing about this trust with their better understanding of emotions and nurse back to health our badly battered and bruised world. How we miss the love showered by women in old societies, depicted so beautifully in old movies and songs! Women need to raise their EQs to that level again to prevent humanity from further degradation.

Nowadays, men and women are, however, more busy competing and confronting each other rather than supporting and loving each other. If young men and women are both running after money, who will look after those lovely bundles of emotions called babies who are the very source of life on Earth? Modern society is guilty of hopelessly ignoring children in their blind pursuit of money. Even a general understanding of the feelings of innocent children is absent. How can we even expect this understanding when children of modern nuclear families spend a major part of their day in crèches or daycare centres? These centres can obviously not cater to the ocean of emotions that flows ceaselessly within each child's mind. So, the emotional connection between adults and children is very low in modern societies.

Social media also gobbles up a lot of time that children could have spent with their parents. And to top it, there are so many social media influencers nowadays who are earning millions by targeting the insecurity and innocence of children. Also, there is no dearth of health food brands that are promoting diseases like diabetes among children by dishing out their dangerously sweetened food and drinks as health foods. If parents do not have time from their ultra-busy schedules and children are allowed to be targeted by such greedy monsters day in and day out, the future generation is bound to be hopelessly sick, both in mind and body. Here I would recommend to the parents who are living a fast life to study the childhood of Franz Kafka, one of the most acclaimed writers of the twentieth century, to get an idea about the soft and tender feelings of children that are being crushed by them on daily basis.

Society should be engineered in such a way that women get ample freedom to beautify society by bringing about this crucial understanding for children and building a healthy society. Therefore, women should be spared from this rat race of money, in whatever way possible, in order to keep life and its beauty alive on this planet. Men need to understand that innocence or love expands as power pulls back its fangs and gives them the necessary space.

It is time to give women this space in society at large to build a more humane world.

Another important correction that is long overdue in the modern society is regarding the teaching methodology adopted by us for children. Nature teaches by experience, whereas modern-age humans believe children can be best taught in classrooms. The main problem with the latter system is that students get to know more about their subjects rather than their own self. On the other hand, the old people who have spent so many years of their life on Earth become wise with age and know a lot more about life and its ways. Now, even science testifies to the fact that older people are wiser. Scientific research has shown that two key brain functions viz. processing new information and focusing on what is important in a given situation, improve with age.[34] The wisdom that comes through age is necessary to closely understand the emotional requirements of the complex human machine. Young men and women today have the tendency to undermine and devalue old technologies and run after new ones, like they hardly think twice while abandoning an old smartphone or laptop when a new upgrade comes into the market. Maybe as a result of this habit, they have also started devaluing old people.

Nature never intended to make old people redundant; it's the money driven economy that promotes this attitude. Thus, in order to promote a life aligned with Nature, it is imperative to include the advice of wise old people too in our decision-making processes at the family level as well as at the state level. At the state level, we can take inspiration from the traditional Indian method wherein a few seers were always a part of a king's cabinet. This arrangement will help in reforming the present-day education system and make it more human-centric. We need to seriously think about what kind of global managers are we producing in the classrooms of our high-profile business schools who have brought our world to the verge of a global disaster in the form of climate change.

Climate change is already upon us due to industrialization in Europe and North America in the past, and in China more recently. According to a report of UNDRR (United Nations office for Disaster Risk Management) the proportion of climate-related natural disasters between 2000-2019 almost doubled from the previous two decades. Such disasters claimed 1.23 million lives and levied an economic cost of 2.97 trillion dollars. And 8 of the top 10 countries hit by these disaster events were developing countries from Asia. When the COP27 (27th United Nations Climate Change Conference) was held in Egypt in November 2022, newspaper reports said that developing countries will require at least $1 trillion in energy infrastructure alone by 2030, and up to $6 trillion across all sectors annually by 2050 to mitigate climate change. In addition, annual climate adaptation costs in these economies could reach $300 billion by 2030 and as much as $500 billion by 2050. Further, developing countries are likely to face $290-580 billion in annual 'residual damages' by 2030 and over $1 trillion in damages by 2050 from the impact of climate change that cannot be prevented by adaptation measures.[35]

From where will the money for paying this atrocious cost of so-called development come? And the economic cost and loss of lives are only going to increase with the passage of time. The environmental clock ticking since 2015 is showing that only around 7 years are left for us to put our act together and prevent global warming to cross 1.5° C, beyond which the worst climate impacts will become inevitable.[36] So, it is time for the general public to step in with the sincerity of fighting an independence struggle to free the world from the misdeeds of the immature minds that have brought the world to such a pass in the name of progress.

Tiokasin Ghosthorse, a peace promoter, says, "We must realize this important distinction: We are not defending Mother Earth. We *are* Mother Earth protecting herself."[37] It is time to get extremely serious and do whatever each human being can do to decrease the usage of every device and activity that contributes to an increase in the level of carbon dioxide in the environment. This includes reduced usage of fossil fuels, adopting healthy food habits and switching to a slower lifestyle that is aligned with

Nature. Food causes 26% of greenhouse gas emissions[38], so choosing the right kind of food is also essential. A slower lifestyle is not all that bad. As explained in this book, it brings with it the gift of love of different hues. Together, these different types of relationships of love will fill your life with joy, and that too at a fraction of the cost compared to the consumer items to which we are addicted nowadays for enjoyment.

The world today is trying to take a number of logical steps required to fight global warming. Efforts are being made to make the world adopt renewable green sources of energy, plant more trees, use energy-efficient bulbs, invent biofuels for aeroplanes, and so on and so forth. However, as long as we don't bring a fundamental change in the way we relate with Nature and all its constituents, we won't be able to succeed. A very constructive step in this direction was recently taken by the Government of India under the able leadership of Prime Minister Narendra Modi with the launch of 'Mission LiFE'. As per the pamphlet of Press Information Bureau, Govt. of India, available online, LiFE stands for 'Lifestyle for Environment'.

Mission LiFE plans to leverage the strength of social networks to influence social norms surrounding climate. The Mission plans to create and nurture a global network of individuals, namely 'Pro-Planet People' (P3), who will have a shared commitment to adopt and promote

Align With the Natural World

environmentally friendly lifestyles. Through the P3 community, the Mission seeks to create an ecosystem that will reinforce and enable environmentally friendly behaviours to be self-sustainable.[39]

It is a fact that adversity is an inevitable part of life, in one form or the other. Many people seek to overcome it by money, some by love and some by both. The last category is the best because excess of everything is bad. Extreme wealth induces an ego and profit-seeking mentality in which no human relationship can remain healthy. Extreme love, on the other hand, can induce in you so much givingness that you may end up as an emotional wreck or a pauper. As pointed out earlier, the ones who follow the middle path and are driven by money as well as love can be called 'Hybrid Humans'.

The world today needs hybrid humans with very sweet will or SWEEET WILL to (S)ave the (W)orld from (E)motional, (E)nvironmental and (E)conomic (T)rauma by (W)isdom, (I)magination, (L)ove and (L)ogic. They should have the requisite commitment to follow this path which may involve sacrificing some monetary benefits to save the planet and their own loved ones.

When Franz Kafka said, "There are two cardinal sins from which all others spring—impatience and laziness"[40], he was actually indirectly advocating for everyone to follow the middle path. When you are impatient, you want to solve a problem as soon as possible without putting in the necessary effort to first understand it. Impatient people love to jump to conclusions. The YOLO approach to life belongs to this category, as discussed in the previous chapter. On the other hand, when you are lazy, you are so slow in tackling the problem that it might never get solved. According to Kafka, both ways are wrong. The best way is to first understand the problem patiently and then solve it at the earliest, which is nothing but the middle path between impatience and laziness.

So, hybrid humans must not rush into providing solutions, like the geeks who are advocating a human-less Earth. In fact, hybrid humans should drag such persons to court for trying to commit the foulest crime against humanity. Similarly, hybrid humans should also not be lazy in implementing well-thought-out solutions, like adopting a slower lifestyle to stop global warming from getting any worse. They should play a very proactive role in working out new solutions using wisdom, imagination, love and logic.

Justin Faerman says, "I see so many people talking about the world's problems but so few talking about the solution to them: Love. It really is that simple… Pretty hard to keep a war going when people are focussed on love. Pretty hard to have an economic crisis when people are cooperating together in love."[41] Hybrid humans have the responsibility to make the world understand that there is an urgent need to change the lifestyle that we have become accustomed to living in the matural world. The time has come to decrease the despicable effects of power and increase love in society at the micro and macro levels to make self-sustaining life possible on this planet.

At the micro or personal level, the matural lifestyle has turned the rule 'opposites attract each other' on its head. The grueling race for money has hardly left anything opposite among the two genders, except the physical appearance. The continuous rant over the equality of power between the two genders has caused a lot of stress in young lives leading to serious damage in relationships. The two genders who should be helping each other out in everyday life are constantly competing with each other due to this narrow view of life, leading to an unprecedented increase in cases of mental stress, marital discords, divorces, suicides, murders and depression. We need to relearn the natural roles of men and women in raising a family that has got blurred because of the unprecedented mix of their roles in this man-made society. As a result of this, the attraction between the two sexes has lost its old-world charm. We need to go to school again to reconnect with Nature and also to connect the future generation with the natural world and all its bounties. School is the best time to inculcate the seeds of love for a lifetime as children can easily relate to emotions.

At the macro level, innovative initiatives from philanthropic institutions and government are needed to enable the weak, the wise and the gentle also to live a life of dignity. Like, governments worldwide can create a Love Fund in which people and corporates contribute and get love certificates or 'Lovies' in return to show their commitment to love towards the planet and its environment. The Ministry of Love will manage all these lovies and spend the money so generated on green projects and to remove poverty, inequality and injustice from society. As pointed out before, work done in this direction should also be counted when we measure the progress of a nation through such numbers as GDP. Ehsaan Masood, author of *GDP, The World's Most Powerful Formula And Why It Must Now Change* while writing in *Science* says, "The numbers are heading in the wrong direction. If the world continues on its current track, it will fall well short of achieving almost all of the 17 SDGs (Sustainable Development Goals) that the UN set to protect the environment and end poverty and inequality by 2030."[42]

Eco-philosopher Henryk Skolimowsiki has proposed a healthy nature-aligned alternative to capitalism and communism, the two major politico-economic systems ruling the world for a long time.

He says, "Present economics has been a handmaiden of capitalism." He calls this alternative system 'Compassionalism'. Compassion for all flora and fauna will be the basis of this economic system, unlike the present system in which the exploitation of Nature is the basis of economic development.[43]

Reviving the sense of love and compassion in society will:

1. Slow down the rat race by making the two sexes complement each other rather than compete with each other. This will promote a joint family culture where the husband, wife, children and elders stay together as a family.
2. Bring down stress and hate levels at the micro and macro levels because of an increased understanding of fellow humans rather than machines. This will lead to a decrease in the need to confront each other with material riches and weapons.
3. Transform the present consumerist societies into holistic societies wherein the welfare of the environment is considered at par with the welfare of humans.

All this will have a salutary effect on the reduction of greenhouse emissions by reducing the demand for fuel, housing, weapons, wasteful consumer items and their even more wasteful upgrades, mass killing of animals for human food, and so on. It will be easier for such a society to adopt green measures by choice and save the world from the emotional, environmental and economic trauma that is waiting in the wings to strike us anytime now.

Appendix

प्यार का महत्व
विपिन मल्होत्रा

प्यार ही है जीने का सहारा,

प्यार से अपना लगे जग सारा,

प्यार ही जीने की चाह जगाऐ,

प्यार ही उसे फिर और बढ़ाऐ।

इस जग में प्यार से वंचित रह जाए जो बेचारा,

जीवन बन जाए उसका इक बोझ, हो जाए वो बेसहारा,

दुनिया की तमाम बहारें लगे उसे फिर फीकी,

उसकी अपनी साॅंसें दुष्मन हो जाऐं उसीकी।

जीवन हो जाऐ उसका वीरान,

जग सारा उसे लगे शमशान,

जीने की वज़ह की वो करे तलाश,

भटके वो जैसे हो जिन्दा लाश।

Appendix

इसीलिए तो किसी ने सच कहा है,

प्यार है पूजा और प्यार खुदा है।

प्यार बेकार नहीं है, ये जरूरत है हर इंसान की,

इसी से आती है चेहरे पे रौनक, और मन में शान्ति।

प्यार के बल पे इठलाऐ ये जीवन धारा,

प्यार न हो तो इंसान हो जाऐ बेचारा,

प्यार से ही कायम है इस जग में आशा,

प्यार न हो तो जीवन बन जाऐ तमाशा।

प्यार के रिशते ही बुनियाद हैं इस संसार की,

भुलादे जो इन रिशतों को, जिन्दगी लगे उसे पहाड़ सी,

प्यार की इस छतरी से मिलती है वो ठण्डी छाया,

जिसकी कामना सदियों से, हर इंसान करता आया।

और कहां तक सुनाऊँ दोस्तों, तुम्हें मैं प्यार की शान,

बस इतना समझ लो, प्यार है हम सबकी जान,

भूलकर भी प्यार की ना कभी करना तौहीन,

क्योंकि प्यार से ही बनती है, ये दुनिया हसीन।

Notes

Chapter 1

1. *Why what we do not know really matters, Times of India (TOI) dt. 06/05/23*
2. *Sacred Space, TOI dt. 28/01/23*
3. *The Speaking Tree, TOI dt. 22/02/23*
4. *https://www.youtube.com/watch?v=aE7rNoO90VI_*
5. *The Speaking Tree, TOI dt. 11/04/23*

Chapter 2

6. *Times Global, TOI dt. 10/10/23*
7. *Times Global, TOI dt. 03/04/23*

Chapter 3

8. *Masculinity is at the root of male violence, TOI dt. 14/01/23*
9. *The Speaking Tree, TOI dt. 28/05/23*
10. *Times Global, TOI dt. 16/02/23*
11. *Grow up, Boys, TOI dt. 24/06/23*
12. *Why what we do not know really matters, TOI dt. 06/05/23*

Chapter 4

13. *The Speaking Tree, TOI dt. 09/07/23*

Chapter 5

14. *The Speaking Tree, TOI dt. 09/07/23*

Chapter 6

15. *Mindfield, TOI dt. 14/01/23*
16. *Mindfield, TOI dt. 14/01/23*

Chapter 7

17. *How anger can affect your body and health, TOI dt. 15/01/23*

Chapter 8

18. *The Speaking Tree, TOI dt. 12/01/23*

Chapter 9

19. *Believe it or not, Delhi Times, TOI dt. 31/03/23*
20. *Why rich people don't just stop working, TOI, October 2019*
21. *Graffiti, Delhi Times, TOI dt. 19/06/23*
22. *Why rich people don't just stop working, TOI, October 2019*
23. *Nature didn't want us to be always happy, TOI, 2019*
24. *Loneliness now a health epidemic in US: 'As deadly as daily smoking', TOI dt. 03/05/23*
25. *The Speaking Tree, TOI dt. 15/01/23*
26. *www.oxfam.org/en/press-releases dt. 16/01/23*
27. *The Speaking Tree Supplement, TOI dt. 22/06/14*
28. *The Speaking Tree, TOI dt. 23/02/23*
29. *www.businesstoday.in (accessed on 02/11/23)*

Chapter 10

30. *Sapiens, A Brief History of Humankind*, by Yuval Noah Harari, p-172-74
31. *The Speaking Tree, TOI dt. 24/04/23*
32. *The Speaking Tree, TOI dt. 25/04/23*
33. *AI and the future of work, TOI dt. 09/06/23*
34. *Older and, yes, wiser. Science says so, TOI dt. 03/11/23*
35. *COP 27 by Samir Saran, TOI dt. 30/10/22*
36. *https://climateclock.world/ (accessed on 02/11/23)*
37. *The Speaking Tree, TOI dt. 15/11/22*
38. *Times Evoke, TOI dt. 22/04/23*
39. *https://www.niti.gov.in/life*
40. *www.goodreads.com /quotes/219408-there-art-two-cardinal-sins-from-which-all-others-spring*
41. *www.awakin.org /v2/read/view.php?tid=2561*
42. *The Speaking Tree, TOI dt. 15/11/22*
43. *The Speaking Tree, TOI dt. 04/05/23*

A Note on the Author

Vipin Malhotra graduated in mathematics from Delhi University. After a long career in Finance, he switched over to publishing and worked in the editorial departments of some renowned global publishers for over a decade, creating textbooks for school students. Nowadays he spends his time researching and writing books and articles on mathematics and social topics.

He can be reached at www.hybridhumans.co.in

www.ingramcontent.com/pod-product-compliance
Lightning Source LLC
LaVergne TN
LVHW041939070526
838199LV00051BA/2840